KW-363-507

Israel's Babe

Anne Bailey

ff
faber and faber
LONDON · BOSTON

by the same author

SCARS
BURN UP
RHYTHM AND BLUES

To
My sister, Sue Burke,
and her husband, Bill.
For all your love.

First published in 1991
by Faber and Faber Limited
3 Queen Square London WC1N 3AU

Photoset by Parker Typesetting Service, Leicester
Printed in Great Britain by Clays Ltd, St Ives plc

All rights reserved

© Anne Bailey, 1991

Anne Bailey is hereby identified as author
of this work in accordance with Section 77
of the Copyright, Designs and Patents Act 1988

A CIP record for this book
is available from the British Library

ISBN 0 571 16243 6

1

'You're going to be all right, Carrie? I mean that. I mean, you know, I'll worry about you.'

'I know you will, Dad, but I'll be okay.'

'Israel seems a long way away.'

'I'm eighteen.'

'You're young.'

'You're a detective, Dad. You only see the bad things.'

'I know I do. I'm protective towards you. I have to be. You haven't got a mother.'

'You're my mother as well as my father, you know that. I mean my friends' dads don't talk about periods or sex or their latest fling. Girlfriends, you know. You're a detective, Dad.'

'Zoe will miss you.'

'And I've been her mother, I know.'

'Well, you have helped me.'

'She's sixteen now. She'll survive. Don't worry, okay?'

Dad smiled at me, then looked at his watch. It was ten o'clock. Time for him to go to the police station or the nick. It would be the last time I saw him. The last time before I flew off to Israel. I was going out there to work on a kibbutz for a while. It was the first time I'd ever been away from home. But it was good for me. The challenge. The expectation. Israel. There is something special about that word. Something special and, with the wars going on, something horrific as well. I wanted to touch it. I wanted to feel it.

Something special. A holiday. A rest. I'd just finished my A-Levels. Dad wanted me to go on to college but I was sick of studying. I rather wanted to do something outrageous like starting my own detective agency. Dad would rather I join the police force, do it all professionally, so to speak. I just knew I couldn't stand another taped-up system. Besides, I'm too headstrong to take any orders from anyone. Perhaps that's because life has taught me to be independent. Still, there you go, that's my dream, to start my own agency. It would be the best detective agency though. The best one in the whole land. Actually my uncle has already promised that I could use a barn on his farm as an office. If I gave him ten pound a week. Now that was something. To have an office. And, oh, what a grand office it would be. How grand. How unique. And I would solve all the world's crime. Brilliant. Dreams come true you know. I think so. I really do.

First I will go to Israel. I will miss Dad and Zoe, but Zoe I will hold constantly in my heart. I shall take all my art stuff. Everything. My easel, my boards, my paints. I mean artists have to do something before they become famous, no one gives them anything. I want to be Van Gogh, or Picasso. Why think small? Being a private detective would leave me enough time to paint. In your own business you can work exactly when you want. The rest of the time could be spent painting. Brilliant.

'Carrie?'

I turned away from the blazing log fire. Turned round to see Dad with his leather jacket on, ready to go. I just smiled at him. We were never one for goodbyes in our family. But, it was kind of hard just then. Knowing he wouldn't be around.

'Carrie, don't forget. You know where I am.'

I went over to him. Just stood in front of him. He reached out and touched my hair.

'Carrie, what you do when you come back. Well, it's up to you, okay? I won't put any pressure on.'

'I know you won't, Dad. I'm going to think about it, all right?'

He kissed me on the cheek. 'See you when I see you.'

'Take care, Dad. I will be thinking of you.'

'Yeah. Bye, love.'

'Dad?' When he was just about to go out of the door. He turned round.

'Keep on catching the bastards, Dad.'

He winked at me. 'Will do.' Then he disappeared. I flopped down on the chair putting my legs over the arm.

'Carrie?'

'You all right, Zoe?'

'I bought you a leaving present.' She walked into the room with her cotton, teddy bear, tee-shirt-like nightie on.

'You shouldn't have spent your money on me, love.'

'It's important to me, Carrie.'

'Come on, then.'

She came across to me and handed me a small package. Just a tiny box done up with Sellotape. I undid the tape and opened the box.

It was a ring, a plain, gold band with a heart on the front. Engraved on the heart were my mother's initials. The tears which had just been threatening earlier came to me fully then. Just a few.

'Well,' she said 'I guess its something Mum would have done if she was still here. And I guess Dad would have done it too if he had the time.'

I smiled. Reached out and touched Zoe's blonde hair.

'Put it on, Carrie. On your little finger. Thats where Dad wears his.'

I did as she said. It fitted perfectly. Zoe smiled and sat down on the settee.

'Don't!', she said, just as I was about to speak. 'I know you're going to lecture me but I don't need it. I don't need it, Carrie. I'm not eight years old any more.'

'I mean, Dad. He'll be out more than he's in.'

'Oh, I've been praying that he'll meet someone. That he'll get married. I always loved Maddi. God knows if they're just friends or what.'

'I'll light a candle on it.' I winked at her.

'You mean next time you're in a Catholic Church.'

'Yeah,' I smiled.

'Dad's an out and out atheist.'

'Oh, I know he stands no chance of getting to heaven.'

'Let's not argue about religion.'

'Quite right. Let's not.'

'You are going to Israel though.'

'I don't know enough about religion to argue about it.'

'Do you think you'll find a boyfriend out there?'

'I might even find a husband, who knows?'

'A husband! You still want to get married and have kids? I thought I'd put you off that idea. Anyway you're really going out there to paint.'

'I want to capture some of it on canvas, yes.'

'So, there'll be no time for boyfriends.'

'Wouldn't you like a brother?'

'I sometimes wish you were a brother. Whenever I wish that I look at your boobs. No, it's true.'

'Yeah, all right, Zoe. You've shocked me, okay?'

'Nothing can shock you.'

'Well, Zoe, I really have got to turn in. The taxi's coming at five in the morning.'

'I won't be up,' Zoe looked down at her hands. 'When will you be back?'

'My ticket's open for a year.'

She tried not to look dismayed but I could see it in her eyes.

'I don't know, Zoe. A couple of months maybe.'

'I'm sorry. I made you say that.'

'We can write. I'll send you the address as soon as I get out there.'

'Yeah, okay. Good luck, then. And if you find a husband he'd better be good-looking.'

'I'll look out for one who can be a good brother to you. Okay?'

'Okay. I'll see you.' She smiled. 'Bye, then.'

It was hard just leaving. Just walking out and not even kissing her. But, I guess, that's how Dad had brought me up. Not to be sentimental. It's a hard world. It really is a hard world.

When I was waiting for the taxi the next morning, I found an envelope on the table with my name printed on it. I recognized Zoe's immaculate writing. I opened the envelope. There was a piece of paper in there with a few words:

I LOVE YOU, CARRIE. I WOULDN'T CHANGE YOU FOR ANYTHING OR ANYONE.

I folded the note and put it in my bag.

Then the taxi came. Before I stepped outside, I had one last look back at the house. Just one last look. And then I was away. First stop. Israel, I thought.

First step, Israel.

2

I wasn't the only one going to the kibbutz. There were other English people too. But me? I just wanted to be alone. I'm the most unsociable person alive. I didn't like the look of the others anyway. All except for a girl who was sitting on her own like me. You know, when we got on the plane she was behind me and I rather hoped she would sit in a smoker next to me. She looked really cool and with it. Different. Eccentric. No show. No falsehood. No rubbishy, shitty normality. And I noticed something. I noticed her cross. Her silver cross with a ruby in the middle of it.

She did sit next to me. I guess by her eyes I knew she'd been watching me too. I knew I'd found a friend. The minute she put her walkman 'phones on and turned it on loud enough so that I could hear the Rolling Stones, 'Get down, baby.' That is what we're talking about, isn't it?

'What's your name?' she asked, after about an hour's flying time.

'Carrie. What's yours?'

'Samantha.'

'Fox?'

'I know I'm well endowed but my surname is Godfry.'

'Godfry? That sounds a posh name.'

'My old man's a doctor.'

'Oh, one of those. My dad's a detective.'

'How old are you?'

'Eighteen.'
'I'm twenty-five.'
'Why are you going?'
'I just wanted a break.'
'Are you a doctor too?'
'No. My big brother is.'
And then I suddenly thought of sibling rivalry. Sibling rivalry. Maybe it was because Samantha had spoken the way she had. Her tone of voice. Big brother, eh. Sometimes I'd dreamt of having a big brother. But then perhaps I would have hated to have a big brother, if that were the truth. Who knows? It's just that when I have kids I want a boy first and then a girl. Just so that the girl can have a big brother.
'What're you thinking?' She turned and smiled at me. She didn't look twenty-five. She only looked about my age. But there was something about her. Some sort of inner confidence. Some sort of peace. I didn't know why it was but I felt very comfortable with her. It was just as if there was no hassle about us. Just as if we both took each other for what we were. Each one of us. No illusions. No snobbery. Friends? I guess some friends are your enemies really. But, with Sam? With Sam, well I just trusted her. From that first meeting I trusted her.
'Oh, I'm just daydreaming,' I said.
'Will they come true?'
'You sound really serious about that.' And it was my turn to smile then.
'That's what dreams are for.'
'To come true?'
'Of course.'
'Actually, I was thinking about babies.'
'Oh, Christ!'
'What's wrong?'

'I'm a confirmed spinster.'

I laughed at her then. I didn't reckon she could ever be termed a spinster. 'Don't you want to get married then?' I asked her, reaching in my bag for the packet of fags I had somewhere.

'Oh, I don't know about ever. Maybe I will. Maybe I won't. But I definitely don't dream about it. You must want to have a baby.'

'I would like a baby, yes.'

'Have you got a boyfriend?'

'No, not at the moment.'

'But there's always a chance. I'm going to have to keep you locked away on the kibbutz. You're a pretty girl, you know.'

'Thanks.'

'And I wasn't flattering you either. I believe in telling the truth. Whatever it is.'

'Not that I want to get pregnant straight away but I do want to be a young mother. That seems important to me, somehow.'

'Have you got a mother?'

'No. She died seven years ago. But that's got nothing to do with it. I'm not hung up about it.'

'My mother went off with another fella. I *am* hung up about it, I hate her. But that can't be true. Who can possibly hate their own mother?'

'I'm sorry.'

'She never wanted a daughter. And that's the truth. She loves my brother. So, what of it? I'm my own person.'

'What work do you do?'

'Basically I've just been dossing. Staying at Uni. Getting into any college that will have me. I don't know what the damn hell I want to do. Dad thought it was a good idea that I come to Israel. Just maybe it'll make my mind up one way or the other.'

'Haven't you got any ambitions?'

'Oh, my ambitions are too way out. Too way out for young ears like yours. And I'm not putting you down either.'

'I know you're not.'

'Oh well. Life goes on, or so they say. Yeah, I will have a fag, if you're offering.'

I gave her a fag, lit my own then we both settled back in silence. I looked out of the small round window and saw the clouds. The white balls of cotton wool. Billowing. Moving. Feathers. Feathers of a bird. Where is heaven? I wondered. This is sky. Heaven must be somewhere. And what about the ozone layer? Really. Oh God, it's a world apart. And I'm flying away from England now. I'm definitely flying away from England. Flying away from my only home. It was a good feeling. Like going on some great adventure. All on my own. To see something different. Different people. Different scenery. And, was I hoping? Was I hoping to meet a guy out there? Was I? Well, who knows. I had dreamt of meeting a guy in Israel. He'd be more of a man, though. About forty. Oh, I know I'm only eighteen but I've always got bored with boys around my age. I wanted someone who would be able to lead me. Like a knight in shining armour. Is that too slushy to think about? Well, I've always gone after the unobtainable. But that was my secret dream and no one could possibly wake me up from that one. No one could possibly. Or so I hoped. So I hoped.

3

I couldn't help feeling a bit nervous when we had to buckle our seat belts and put our fags out to be ready for landing. Sam was asleep and I had to nudge her awake. The time had gone quite quickly on the plane really. Sam and I had played a quiz game she'd brought. It was a travelling one so that got our brains in order just a bit. In fact, all in all, Sam and I had become really good friends. I was glad I'd found her because everyone else had seemed to pair off as well. Or be in groups or something.

'We're landing.' I spoke as she rubbed the sleep out of her eyes.

'We are? What's the time?'

'Eleven-thirty.'

'So, this is it, then. The big unknown.'

'Yeah. We're here.'

Both Sam and I strained to look out of the window as the plane was landing. It was amazing. Just a vast amount of arid desert. With only patches of greenery here and there. It was amazing. It really was. To actually arrive. Arrive in Israel. That land. That special land. It was special. It was special to me. Israel was special and I could sense that Sam felt the same way too. The Holy Land. Well it all happened there. It all happened. I was quite overwhelmed really. As the plane actually touched down, in a strange way I felt like crying.

It was all around us. The unceasing desert. The cacti. The sun scorched lands. This is the land. And we saw the army vehicles. We saw soldiers as we walked across the tarmac. Soldiers to greet us. Their weapons held grimly. This is the land of the wars. Well, of course it is. Perhaps it has always been the land of the wars. Ever since Christ was born. Ever since then. I wished then, I just wished then that I had studied the history of Israel. That I knew more about it. I mean really I didn't know what the war was about, which is pretty ignorant of me. It was just different people with different religions. Fighting each other. God knows what it was all about really. I just hoped we wouldn't get blown up or shot or something. And even that thought was quite exciting really.

We managed to collect our luggage and then went out through the terminal where a coach was waiting for us all. It was a unique experience. I just couldn't get over the scenery. There were mountains in the distance. Mountains and I felt like getting my painting stuff out and painting on my first impressions. I couldn't. We walked on to the coach and found a place. We were both silent then. Trying to take in everything. Neither of us wanted to miss a thing. The coach began rolling and we knew then we were just hours away from the kibbutz. From our kibbutz which was near the Gaza Strip.

It was weird, it was like a culture shock in a way. It was all so different. The sun was beating down and it was hot in the coach. All around us there were still deserts. Spasms of land reaching far beyond and further. The main road we were on wasn't like a main road in Britain. It was smaller, narrower. It didn't have white lines down the middle and the coach driver was going fast. It was hard to take it all in at once. I had imagined what it would be like but I'd never imagined anything as sparse looking. As barren. There were large cacti growing along the way. Large beastly looking things. It was just like cowboy land. That's what I thought. Like the cowboy land you saw on Westerns on TV.

This guy, Don, introduced himself to us. He was the guy who took care of all the volunteers who came to work on the kibbutz. He gave us some general information as to what would be happening when we arrived and then he told us a bit about himself. He'd come to the kibbutz when he was nineteen and had been there for ten years. After a year he'd been accepted as a member of the kibbutz and after three years took on this job of looking after the newcomers. He told us he expected reasonable behaviour at all times and that the kibbutz committee had the right to chuck anyone off the kibbutz if they caused undue trouble. There were to be no drugs brought on to the kibbutz. If we smoked we would receive twenty cigarettes a day as our quota from the kibbutz. We would receive a card on arriving which would have our allowance written on it. There would be no cash transactions on the kibbutz. Everything would be written on this card. When we had to buy something from the shop we would take the card in and get the money deducted from that. Each week we would have a certain amount put on. Not much, but enough to buy essentials.

Don came round and collected our insurance papers and anything else we wanted to keep in the safe, so Sam and I decided to keep our passports and travellers cheques in there too for safekeeping. He then told us a bit about the work available to us and that we would work on a rota basis, in one place for a few days or weeks then we would be moved on to something different. He said they had a very nice factory which made ball valves and they grew oranges on the kibbutz which needed to be harvested. There was also a chicken farm and a place where they needed two people to cook meals for six men. That would be at a place out of the kibbutz. There were jobs clearing the communal dining hall and working in the kitchens as well. Don told us there would be a work sheet in the dining hall and each week we would look at it to see where we would be working on each day.

'It's no good me telling you much else. We're nearly there now, so I'll show you around when we arrive and get settled. First we'll sort out where you'll be living. After I've shown you around you'll have the rest of the evening free. They've arranged for some food to be laid on in the dining hall. So, if you're there at about half-past seven you'll get those stomachs full. Tomorrow will give you a chance to settle in as it's Saturday. No one works on a Saturday. It's their Sabbath. So, you'll be starting work on Sunday.'

The only way I could describe the kibbutz was like a sort of castle in the middle of a desert. Well, not really a castle, because it wasn't just one large building but it was like an island. We had to go through an armed guard and Don told us the kibbutz was surrounded by barbed wire. We'd be issued with passes to get in or out.

'Christ!' Sam said, 'It's like a prison camp.'

'It does look like a prison.'

We drove through the gates and suddenly we were hit by greenery. Green fields. Green trees which I didn't know the names of. Tropical looking trees, though. There were small white buildings in rows and Sam spotted the large swimming pool as we passed it.

'Now, to the left as we pass is the dining hall,' Don was saying. 'That's where we have all our meals. And where important kibbutz decisions are made. The laundry is just behind it to the left. We'll be stopping shortly.'

It was amazing to actually climb out of the coach and be on the kibbutz. We stopped in front of a plain field with a row of shack-like buildings to our right. There was a small group of people to welcome us and they shook our hands and asked our names.

'Now,' Don clapped his hands for silence. 'First of all let's get the accommodation sorted out. There's only two single huts and the others are twos and threes. I'll leave you all to get on with that. Any of these two rows up here and it bears round to your left. If you can just dump your stuff in your rooms and meet me back here in about ten minutes.'

There was slight turmoil as everyone made a dash for their belongings. When Sam and I found everything we wandered off in the direction Don had said. We went in the first shack which happened to be empty.

'This is for two,' Sam said. 'It's a bit barren isn't it. There's not even a carpet.'

'We haven't booked into the royal plaza you know.'

'Well, I guess this is home then,' she said, banging her rucksack down on the bed which was across one wall of the room.

'I'll have this one then,' I said, dumping my own luggage as well as all my painting gear. Dumping it down and thinking, well this is it, this is really going to be home. Sam was right, though. It was all pretty sparse. Just two beds which hadn't been made up. Just two beds, two small bedside cupboards, and there was actually one wardrobe with a cracked and rusting mirror on the door.

'We've got five minutes,' Sam said. 'There isn't even a proper door, I hope there's no awful insects about.'

There was also a wash basin in the corner but when I tried the hot tap nothing came out of it. There was no proper door. Just a curtain which could be pulled back and forth. But thinking about it, perhaps it got too hot for a proper door.

'Well, they don't go to much expense, do they?' I said. 'I'm going to hunt out the showers.'

'Don't forget we've got to meet Don.'

I didn't forget we had to meet Don and in fact we were the first ones there. Anyway, after about fifteen minutes when everyone had turned up he began his tour of the place.

It took about three-quarters of an hour for him to show us around. He showed us the main places. Like the dining hall. It was a large, airy place. With the sun shining on it. It consisted of long tables running the length of the hall. Then we went out and had a look at the chicken farm. Don told us you had to take a shower before you went in and a shower when you came out and you had to wear special clothes. But the showers were just in the entrance to the chicken farm. It all looked rather different and spectacular. Actually it made me hope that I would be working in there. Collecting all the eggs from the birds. Anyway, then we went on round to the swimming pool which was fenced in. And then to the laundry where we could do all our washing. Then we walked down dirt tracks and across green patches to the houses of the people who actually lived on the kibbutz. Don quickly showed us his home, which consisted of a bedroom, a lounge, a shower and a small kitchenette-type place. Actually he had like rubber dolls hanging up and all sorts of ancient relics in his place. It rather reminded me of black magic. You know, like the dolls you stick pins into. But that was just my imagination running away with me. I was sure Don couldn't really be into black magic. We walked on and came to the factory. It was small and airy. With clean table tops. It didn't seem like a factory at all. Not like the large, horrible factories you got at home. This wasn't so bad. Not so bad at all. He showed us what they made there and introduced us to the factory manager who was an Israeli called Yacombe or something like that.

There was a special room where you could sit and read or play games. There was also a cinema which showed films every Friday and Saturday night and that was completely free. You didn't have to pay. He said they showed English films mainly. There were four tennis courts where you could hire things to play tennis and near the cinema there was a hall with table tennis tables in it and like a small gymnasium which we could use at any time. There was also a running track and a football pitch. Really, there was much more on the kibbutz than I'd thought there'd be.

'Well, it's going to take some time for you to get to know your way around properly but I've shown you most of what you need to know at first. If ever you want to see me you'll find me in the office just to the right of the laundry. That's my place and we can sort things out if there are any problems. The doctor comes here twice a week and if you need to see him at all I can arrange that for you. If you'd like to find out more about family life on the kibbutz, it can be arranged that you be adopted by a family and they'll invite you into their home. Well, that's about all for now. There's an hour to go before food will be served so I'll leave you to settle in a bit. Have a wash, etc. Are there any questions before we split?'

A few people asked questions about this and that and afterwards we all meandered away.

'I might do that,' Sam said.

'Do what?'

'Be adopted by a family. First-hand knowledge and all that.'

'God, I feel knackered now.'

'Yeah, I'm feeling it a bit.'

'I might have a shower and get changed for tea.'

'We could go and have a shower together.'

'After dinner we could go to the bar.'

'Yeah.'

'Come on, let's go and have a shower. I feel really shitty.'

The showers and loos were down a track to the right of our shacks. We had to take all our clothes with us to change into. And our soap and shampoo etc. The showers were okay but not that grand. At least they had hot water, that's if you could work the system so that you didn't get boiling hot water or freezing cold water. Sam and I managed to sort it out though. It was bliss to have a shower and wash our hair. Getting all the grime of travelling out of our bodies. Washing all the dirt away. It made us feel less tired too. It was so hot outside it didn't matter about going out with wet hair. Sam wore shorts and I wore one of my skirts. Then we collected our stuff together and made our way back. We were glad we'd had a shower then because as we were leaving a group of about five girls were coming to have a shower as well. We said hi to them and then made our way back.

'Well, what d'you think?' Sam asked. 'What d'you really think of this place?'

'I think it's going to be okay. I really do think it's going to be okay.'

'Glad you came then?'

I nodded. 'Are you, then?'

'All I need is a good night's sleep.'

'Tea and then bar first?' I was hoping.

'We'd better unpack.'

'We'll never get an early night.'

'Oh well,' Sam shrugged, 'to hell with an early night. We'll have a long morning instead.'

'Sounds okay to me.'

'Let's go and find out what the food's like then.'

That's what we did. As we were trying to find the canteen again I suddenly felt overwhelmingly happy. A strange, floaty sort of feeling. It felt so great. It really did feel great. I felt independent and free. I really did. Independent and free. That meant something to me then. It meant something. It really did.

4

The dining hall was like a a self-service restaurant. All the food was on trays along one side of the hall as you came in. There was loads of food. All different types. It was like a great big food centre. Consisting of mainly salads. Rice. Pasta. All sorts of mixtures. It was like a cold buffet at a wedding and I, for one, loved that type of food and it all seemed healthy enough anyway. There were different kinds of cold meats and eggs. All we had to do was grab a plate and pile it on. I must say I did make rather a pig of myself. But I was feeling pretty hungry. There were also cups and saucers with urns of tea and coffee.

Sam and I managed to find a small table with no one else at it. We wanted to be alone. Unsociable that we were. There were only a few tables with only four on so we both rather hoped we could stake our claim forever on that particular table which looked out on to a forecourt and a garden.

Sam had picked out rather a plateful of food too. Although she had grumbled about it when first seeing it. I'd begun to realize that Sam moaned about things quite a bit. It was like she had to have a good moan before she could accept something. She did look tired, though. Perhaps that was why she seemed a bit irritable. Anyway, it wasn't anything to worry about and I was too interested in my food to have an in-depth conversation about it.

'Excuse me.'

I looked up. First at Sam and then at the man who had interrupted us.

'I'm very sorry to disturb you but I wondered if I could share your table. It's just that I can't stand being on the large tables and I shouldn't really be here anyway.'

'Of course,' I said, moving over. Sliding my plate across. He was rather a stout man with dark, curly hair. He had a stubble of beard on him as if he hadn't shaved for a couple of days. Actually in spite of all this he looked rather distinguished. Distinguished but nice with it. I mean although he spoke well he wasn't snobbish or anything. I wasn't sure if Sam liked him, though. I thought she looked a little put out and she didn't smile at the man or anything. Just carried on eating her food as he sat opposite her with a plate brimming with food.

Actually it was a bit awkward. I mean this guy was quite good-looking and for a start I rather liked him. You know, he had that air about him. But whenever I fancy anyone I always go into a mega panic when I get too close to them. I get all hot and flustered and don't know what I should say. Well, just then I began to panic, just a bit. Although I did try hard to keep in control of my feelings.

'My name's Clifford,' he suddenly said.

'Oh?' I answered because it didn't look as if Sam was going to and one of us had to. 'I'm Carrie and this is Sam.'

Clifford smiled at Sam but she didn't smile back.

'We're tired,' I said. 'You know, with the travelling. We've only just arrived.'

'Yes, yes. You must be tired.'

'Are you English?' Sam suddenly spoke.

'Yes I am.'

'How long have you been out for?'

'Actually I've been out here six months. I'm working out here.'

'Oh, really? And what is your work?'

'Actually I'm a playwright.'

'Oh, yeah.'

I felt completely and utterly shocked. Sam really seemed to be laying into the man. He's a playwright, well, I hadn't missed that. And I hadn't missed how Sam was behaving either.

'I am a professional playwright,' he said, seeming to suddenly pull himself together. In fact his eyes, I thought, held a spark of indignation.

'Telly?' Sam spoke again.

'Telly. Theatre. Oh, you'll find my name in all the good magazines.'

'You mean, like *Vogue*?' Sam actually smiled and she seemed to have lost that hostility she had held for him.

'In all the top magazines actually.'

'Yeah, I thought I recognized you. I studied one of your plays at college. The modern playwright. Well, not so much the modern. Yeah, I've got your features etched on my brain and *The Urge to Cry*, as well.'

'Well, I thought you looked like a critic.' Clifford moved his rice around on the plate, without actually eating it. I felt completely out of this conversation but I was listening well. Listening well and observing everything. Especially about Cliff. I liked him. You know, he could be famous. But he didn't act famous. He wasn't big-headed or anything. He was just cool, you know. Really cool and laid back. I really had a feeling for him and I felt like finding out more about him. In a way I thought he was quite good-looking. But brains are better than brawn. And brains are better than looks. The intellectual. Could I really be a private detective and be an intellectual as well? Who knows? But I'm an artist as well. Although I'm not quite famous yet.

'Are you married?' I came out of my dreams to hear Sam's voice once again.

'Married? Yes. Divorced? Yes. It didn't work out. My own failure. She was a childhood sweetheart but then I grew up.'

'It's usually the female outgrowing the man.'

'Well, either way, what matters?'

'How old are you then?' And Sam suddenly winked at me. I knew she'd only done that because I thought it was completely impolite to ask a virtual stranger his age.

'I'm forty. That's the crisis I'm going through now.'

'My friend here, Carrie. She's an artist.'

'An artist?' Clifford looked at me and I thought I saw hope in his eyes then. Hope. But for what? God knows.

'Oh, I don't paint for a living,' I said. Quickly just in case he thought I was a professional like him.

'She's going to paint out here. Pretty powerful stuff isn't it? In Israel.'

'I could take you out to my hideaway,' Clifford spoke, turning to me. And I suddenly noticed his deep blue eyes. 'That's where I go to escape. Some clefts in the middle of the desert. A little hole amidst the rocks. A little cave. My own little cave. No one will have the privilege of seeing it. No one apart from a special person. Don't worry, Carrie. I see panic in you. I just say my prayers there.' Then he smiled. He smiled such a warm smile and his teeth were so white. He smiled at me but I also noticed the wink. The quick wink at Sam. I suddenly felt confused.

Confused somehow. It was almost as if Sam and Clifford had some kind of secret together. I finished my food and suddenly felt slightly grumpy. You know, sensitive, as if the joke was on me.

'We're going for a drink after we've unpacked and made our beds,' Sam spoke. 'In the bar. Will you be there?'

'Yeah, I sometimes have a nightcap over there.'

'Well, we might see you later then.'

'It'll be my pleasure.'

'Come on then, Carrie. We've got things to do.'

I just followed Sam out. I still felt agitated and rather disappointed. In a way I would have liked to have stayed with Clifford. Chatted more to him. By myself. But then Sam had rather overtaken me on that score, I mean it wasn't just that I liked him physically. I was attracted to him mentally as well. He seemed so mature and intelligent, well he must be brainy to be a playwright. I just followed Sam out, though.

'What's wrong?' Sam asked, as we were on our way to the laundry to collect our bed linen.

'Nothing.'

'Oh, come on. I thought we were friends.'

I just shrugged.

'Carrie! Stop a minute.'

'I'm all right,' I said and I kept on walking. But, strangely, I felt close to tears. I suddenly felt as if I wanted a good cry.

'Carrie.' She caught up with me. 'Carrie, you know that guy fancies you.'

I stopped. Looked at her. 'What?'

'He's got an eye out for you. Well didn't you notice?'

I shook my head.

'Well, you're not very observant.'

'He could be my father.'

'So? Do you run from the very thing you want?'

'I don't believe in sex before marriage. If that's all he's after he can fuck off.'

'Christ, you are in a mood.'

'Am I meant to be in a mood just because I don't believe in sex before marriage?'

'I'm not getting at you for that. It's up to you.'

'Well, he's probably just after my body, okay?'

'I think he's after your soul, not your body.'

'Well, forget it.'

'You're tired. I think we'll have an early night.'

'Just because you're older than me it doesn't mean you need to protect me. I'm trying to get away from being protected. That's why I left my home.'

'And how the hell am I meant to be protecting you?'

'I knew damn well he fancied me. That's why he came to the table.'

'Liar.'

We went into the laundry room and grabbed some clean sheets, a blanket and pillow cases.

'It's a big step, you know,' Sam said as we were walking back. 'It's a big step leaving home at your age. You still need friends you know. No one's that independent.'

'I've never had friends. I can do without them.'

'You want me to move out?'

I stopped. Suddenly. Realizing what she'd said. Of course I didn't want her to move out. We were meant to be friends. We really were. Suddenly I started crying.

'It's hard, Carrie. Leaving home. You think it's going to be easy but it's not. You want independence but you don't really realize you've been protected. Not until you get out amongst the wolves. I like you. You know, we're friends. You protect me. I'll protect you.'

I wiped my face with my hands.

'Tomorrow,' she said, hooking her arm through mine. 'Tomorrow we can both write home.'

I smiled. She smiled. Yeah, that seemed okay. Tomorrow we can both write home.

5

I could write home. It was easy to write home the next day without getting too upset. You know, it had just been heavy the night before, after all the travelling. And the meeting new people. A different place. A different life. I guess even the best of us get tired sometimes. Anyway, I didn't wake up until ten in the morning. When I did wake I found Sam in the middle of exercises. It was easy then. It felt so good to wake and realize it had all happened. That I was actually in Israel.

'Well, morning! You've decided to surface, have you?'

I stretched and yawned a morning to Sam.

'It is something,' she said. 'Doing your karate exercises in Israel.'

'Is that what you're doing?'

'Just limbering.'

'You do karate?'

'Yeah, Korean. It's the kicking, boxing kind.'

'Oh, great. Have I missed breakfast?'

''Fraid so. Lunch is in a couple of hours though.'

'Aaaah,' I yawned. 'Guess I can manage until then.'

'Happier this morning, are we?'

'Did we go to the bar last night?'

'No. Reckon we both collapsed in a heap.'

'Well,' I got up and sprung on to my feet. 'Here we are then.'

'We've got to get our airmail writing stuff and some

stamps. We had better write home today.'

'Yeah. They'll be worried about us otherwise.'

'I met this Israeli guy at breakfast. Hiesha. He's got to go to war in three weeks. You know, in the army. He's been called up.'

'That must be awful.'

'Yeah, he said his mother keeps crying every time she sees him.'

'I suppose a lot of them get killed.'

'Actually he's okay. I never saw Clifford down there, though. The man of your life.'

'Oh, sure.' I went to throw a pillow at her but it fell on the floor instead.

'Well, who's to know? Hiesha seems okay, though. He says a lot of volunteers that come here, like us, take drugs apparently.'

'Drugs?' I was really surprised.

'Yeah. We're in the big world now. Anything goes.'

'You wouldn't take any, would you?'

'What the hell do you take me for?' She looked at me with anger glinting in her eyes.

'Well, who does take them then?'

'The rest of the dossers who are here I expect. Anyway, I'll see you later. I'm meeting Hiesha. He wants me to have a run against this other guy on the track.'

I wanted to ask her about the run or whatever but when I tried to she just flapped her arms about. 'Oh, I'll tell you later. I must go. Hiesha will be waiting .'

'Friends, eh?' I said, being sarcastic. As she was on her way out.

'Oh, yeah,' she answered. 'Real good friends,' which just didn't tell me much either way.

After having a wash and getting changed I managed to find Don's office where I managed to get both mine and Sam's money card. Then I went to the shop and bought an airmail pad and envelopes, finishing off with a couple of stamps. When I was on my way back I was looking forward to writing to Dad and Zoe. I felt in a happy mood too. Not at all like last night. Everything seemed so much clearer now than it had done. The sun was shining and the sky was a pastel blue. I spoke to a few people I met but I was aware that drugs were on the horizon somewhere and that just wound me up to think about it. I mean, why spoil the whole place and experience by taking mind-blowing drugs. It was crazy. I just didn't understand people like that. I really didn't. Still, not to worry. I'm here in Israel and I know I'm not going to spoil it all. I'm not going to spoil it at all.

I spent a long time writing home. It was a long letter. All about our flight, our kibbutz and I even told them about Clifford. Oh, I said, there are lots of eighteen-year-olds here. They're a bit like the girls at school who used to bully me a lot. In fact I believe I really could get into a fight or two. I can see it coming. I guess some people just hate me from the outset. Perhaps because I hate them. Who's to know, the proverbial loner is me. But I have made a friend. I've made a very good friend in Sam. (A girl by the way.) Just in writing about Sam I knew would cheer Dad and Zoe up. Make them easier about me being so far away. I mean everyone likes a friend, don't they? Everyone likes a friend. Anyway I managed to finish the letter putting tons of kisses at the bottom and then I sealed it and put the stamp on ready to post.

I took my easel out of its special box I'd brought, along with the rest of my art stuff. It had survived the journey. So in the end I was glad I'd decided to lug it all over, after all. Actually, I felt quite inspired. Well, who knows? Great aspirations in Israel!! Someone was inspired once. And anyway I'm not even religious. That's if you call going to church religious. Well, I don't go to church so that counts me out. Anyway I didn't really know why I was thinking such things. I guess it's just being in Israel. Some history. Really. I wished I'd stuck my Bible in too. But Sam would have probably laughed me out of town if I'd brought that particular book along. Oh well, I set my easel up and slipped my painting shirt over my tee shirt. It all fitted in to the space at the bottom of my bed and it was near the window so the light seemed okay to work in. A large painting pad was in order so I fixed that too. Of course, this is pure illusion. I don't paint your average scenic picture. No. I paint from the power of my feelings. The power of me. The power of my own God. I paint illusions really. Everyone's illusions. Or could you call them hallucinations? Who knows? I see a person and I can paint from their very vibes. I can get so charged up with people. All sorts of people. Then I go mad in a frenzy to get the images from my mind down on paper.

I started working.

'Hells Bells!!'

One hour later Sam came in.

'Christ!' She was shouting. I'd already jumped out of my performing illusion, though, with her first entrance. I definitely got the feeling that she was annoyed with something. Very annoyed.

'Bastards!' She threw her tee shirt away from her body. Just like peeling a banana, I thought.

'I can't do it, Christ.' Then she took off her tracksuit bottoms. I got up and discreetly closed the curtain so nobody had a first-class view.

'Sam?' I had to yell. 'What's wrong?'

'I matched him pace for pace. Pace for pace. I mean that. This really big-headed English guy. Hiesha hates him, He's been such a pig. I had to beat him.'

'What happened then?'

'Oh, nothing. Nothing.' She put on her silk dressing gown and flopped down on her bed. Sweat was dripping off her.

'I never knew you could get so uptight. I wish you'd tell me it all. Every sordid little detail.'

'Oh, he beat me, that's all. He beat me but I had him covered. Right up to the last stretch. I was sure to God I had him covered.'

'So?' I was confused. 'Is that a big deal?'

'I'm down on my time. I mean, God I'm slow. I'm too damn slow. It's my time, Carrie. I should be better.'

'Is this all for karate?'

'Karate and the hundred metres and the decathlon. You're the painter. I'm the athlete. I belong to a club. But when I'm that slow! Christ, I'm practically two minutes down.'

I shrugged. 'Well, it's not a competition, is it?'

'It's competition to me. All my sport is competition.'

'Are you and Hiesha getting together or something?' I wiped my brush on my painting shirt.

'Is that all you can think about? Be nice to a guy and you think I want to have a relationship with him. God, go and bury your head in the bloody desert,' she spat at me.

'Okay. Don't get so phased.'

'I didn't make it, Carrie. Can't you see that? I haven't made it. I haven't worked hard enough. I'm not an athlete. I didn't have the guts to get to the Olympics. Just self-satisfaction. I think of what I missed. What I could have done. Instead of fighting Dad all the time. Instead of fighting my brother. Carrie, I came out to Israel for one thing. To find a life. My life. I didn't tell you but I've got no mother either. I love my Dad. I do. Oh, what the hell. I don't know what the hell I want to do with my life. This English guy winds me up because he's going to America to train. At one of the athletic colleges over there. Christ, Carrie, I'm twenty-five and I've done nothing with my life. Nothing. Just dossed.'

I put my paintbrush down and just as I turned back to Sam I saw two feet appear underneath our curtain and then head a voice.

'Excuse me.'

I knew the voice. It was Clifford. I knew straight away. My heart missed a beat. I looked at Sam but she just turned her head away, burying it in the pillow. I pulled back the curtain.

'Hello,' he said, looking rather scruffily clad. With hair sticking up in all the places which it shouldn't. As if he'd just had an electric shock or something.

'Hello,' I didn't know what else to say really and there was a kind of embarrassed silence for a while between us.

'Well,' he suddenly smiled, looking more at ease. 'How are you, Carrie?'

I couldn't help smiling. He looked so bloody innocent. Rather dashing, though. A right gentleman, I thought.

'I wondered if you would like me to show you to the swimming pool. Then, perhaps this afternoon we could both have a swim.'

'Look, come in. It's awkward standing there.'

'I rather thought Sam was a bit cross. I saw her about ten minutes ago. She just walked straight past me without a word.'

'Don't worry. It's nothing to do with you. Come on in.'

'Don't worry, Clifford,' Sam yelled. 'I'm decent. Come in and join the happy throng.'

When Clifford came in he walked straight away to my first masterpiece in Israel. He made no comment though and just sat down on my bed.

'Well, we really can't offer you anything to drink,' I said.

'Yes, it does seem a bit barren. At least they've given me a kitchen.'

'So, next shout's on you, is it?' Sam actually pulled herself from her bed. Showing far too much leg for a man's company, I thought. But then, I do tend to be a bit prudish sometimes. Well, that's what Zoe tells me, back home.

'Yes, of course, of course.' Clifford stood up. Just as if he had to. Sam was hunched on her bed, covering her legs with a sheet. I was just standing behind Cliff when he turned round and looked at me.

'Really,' he started. 'Would you like to come and have a look around? It may even give you time to catch up on inspiration. If you feel the same creative forces that I do.'

'Why don't you take her to your hideaway in the desert?' Sam said, reaching for her fags and lighting one. 'Pass the ashtray, Carrie. Have one if you want.'

'No. No, really. I am trying to give up or at least cut down.'

'So, are we going?' Clifford said. 'Would you like to come too, Sam?'

'No. Thanks all the same. I'll leave you two to reap

out inspiration where you can. Getting vibes from the barbed wire around the kibbutz, I presume. Well, all I hope is that you've both left me plenty of dough in your wills.'

'Oh, darling. You need not be so pessimistic,' Cliff said, reaching out and touching Sam's head. 'You really must be a great athlete.'

'Oh God, you weren't watching were you?'

'Oh God, you're right. I was watching in fact.'

'Well, in that case the ship was definitely sinking.'

'Not with that young gentleman, I presume. It looked as if it was full steam ahead.'

'Piss off you two. Let me feel sorry for myself in peace.'

'You must come swimming with us too, this afternoon.'

'Really, Clifford. I didn't hear Carrie saying she was going swimming with you. Although I could have sworn she wants someone to tell her what to do.'

'Come, Carrie.' Clifford held out his hand, 'Come on.'

I followed him. I didn't take his hand but I followed him. I felt so proud though. Just to be walking with him. He had on brown cords with a whiter than white shirt which really showed up his dark skin and dark features. I could hardly believe it was actually happening. When he suddenly took my hand I thought I was going to faint or something. But I tried desperately to hold on to reality. I could feel his short stubby fingers against my own though and they were so strong. Strong and sure, I thought. Strong and sure. I couldn't help imagining him being a playwright.

I mean I thought about it and didn't really have to

imagine because it was the truth. And for such an important person to want me. Just the thought took my breath away. I was stuck for words in fact. Because of the importance of it all, especially when he took my hand. But I didn't pull away from him.

'Let's take the weight off our feet.' He walked me into one of the many garden areas which had two white iron chairs in it, not too hard though because they had cushions to sit on.

'This is a pleasant place to sit. Where we can just waste a few hours. I sometimes do a spot of writing out here.'

'You are really a playwright?'

'And you? You're very shy, aren't you?'

'I'd say careful, not shy.'

'I am forty you know.'

'I'm not scared of that. I always wanted to go with an older man.'

'A divorced older man?'

'No one keeps their vows these days.'

'You're right. They don't. But maybe once is enough. Who knows? My first wife wasn't in the art world. In the world of creation. She's a teacher. It didn't work. It really didn't work.'

'How long were you married for?'

'Six years. I've been divorced for five years.'

'Were there any children?'

'I've got a daughter. Just one. We only had Isobelle. I call her Izzy. She hates her name. She's eleven. She wants to be a doctor.'

'Does she live with you?'

'She's with her mum. I see her weekends mainly. When we're both around. I do travel quite a bit though. Well, every two years I spend about six months out here. My parents used to live out here.

They were on a kibbutz. I spent some of my childhood on one. So, it's like in my blood sort of. It gets me away from the pressures of life at times. Somewhere I can just write in peace.'

I was drawing invisible circles on my legs as Cliff was speaking. But I was listening. Listening to every word he said. What mattered? Christ, this is Israel. So? He had an eleven-year-old daughter. What of it? But he'd made no promises. All he'd done was ask me out for a walk, was hold my hand while we walked. I suddenly pulled my hand away from him, though. On a sudden impulse. He looked at me with concern. Perhaps a sign of hurt in his eyes, and then something else. A look of understanding. As if he knew I was afraid, afraid of giving myself to anyone. He seemed to be saying eradicate it. Eradicate your fear. Do that and fall in love with me.

I looked down at my unheld hand. It had been warm. Warm and good. It was like a dream though. Like nothing I had known back in England. This phase of my life. This chapter. I'd suddenly felt engulfed. Been afraid of my very own emotions. Suddenly. For a little while. Just like that. Really, just like that.

6

We didn't go swimming. I spaced out on him. That was a few minutes after I'd pulled my hand away. I just got up and walked away. Walked away from him. I went back to the hut and was glad to find Sam had gone out. I just lay on my bed and thought. I can't handle this, can I? Not this. Not when we're so far away from home. But I needed someone. I've always needed someone. I didn't want to cry but I found tears running down my face and suddenly I thought, to hell with it! I've got to enjoy this. It's Israel. It's my life. My own experience. And meeting a guy like Cliff was all I'd ever dreamt about. Like I'd dreamt about getting married too. Getting married and having babies. But then I suddenly thought of Dad and his reaction. He'd go mad. He'd go mad if I told him I was going out with a forty-year-old man. At the best of times Dad would always suss out my boyfriends. The crazy thing was that if Dad didn't like them, then I would chuck them. Why, I don't know. I mean Dad was always too busy working to get to know any of my boyfriends better. So, anyway, what the hell? I guess I'm still after Dad's approval. I knew one thing, I'd never get it for Cliff.

I painted the rest of the day away and started getting nervous about going down to dinner and seeing Cliff again. Butterflies raged in my stomach. I just tried to take it all out on the paper in front of me.

'For Christ sake! Don't tell me you've been sitting

in here all day. I thought you were going out with Cliff. What's wrong with you? This is Israel babe, it's holiday. You know, it's people and it's fun. Real people, you know. You can talk with them and laugh with them. They're going to think you're an oddball, you know.'

I listened to Sam's words. They just whizzed round my brain, though. Not really finding true meaning.

'I mean, what happened with Cliff?' Sam continued. 'Why did you bother coming to Israel if you're going to do exactly the same things that you did at home. You have to join in with the others you know. Sometimes.'

I still said nothing. I just got up and ran my hands down my painting shirt. I liked my work. It was a picture depicting Christ and the Devil all in one. It was pretty way out but good. I knew that. I said nothing. Just watched Sam walk across the room to the painting. She looked at it. Just stared at it. Her mouth fell open.

'What is this?' She spoke quietly, having dispensed with her yelling.

'What d'you think it is? It's what I've been doing.'

'I mean, God, you didn't . . . I mean, have you ever been to art school?'

'No.'

'Did you do all of this?'

'Of course I did.'

'I'm sorry, Carrie, but I underrated you. And your painting.'

'Oh, don't worry, most people do.'

'You've got to let someone professional see your work, you know.'

'I just thought I might take them to galleries or something.'

'You should, Carrie. You've got something. God knows what, but it's there.'

'Don't go on about it. I felt inspired, that's all.' I moved away from her and took the shirt off.

'Carrie, I'm sorry I had a go at you, okay? I wasn't getting at you. Just that some of the others have been talking about you. You know, I guess they're just being bitchy.'

'Oh, yeah? I've met bitches before. I can handle them.'

We both sat on the edge of my bed.

'I know why now,' Sam said. 'I know why they're trying to stir things. Because you're different, that's why. They haven't got the brains or the talent or the guts to be different. I'll tell you something. If anyone upsets you I'll be after them. I will. I'll drop them to the ground with one fist. I want you to believe that. They're just jealous of you.'

'Do you want a cup of coffee?' I got up and went to the kettle which had been delivered to us with a box containing, mugs, tea and coffee. We had to buy our milk from the shop.

'Yeah. Good idea. Let's have a cup of coffee.'

It was strange really. Sam speaking the way she had. Wanting to protect me. I guess she really cared. She wasn't just faking it. I'd never had a friend who cared like that before. But then I s'pose Sam and I are quite similar in a way.

'Carrie?'

I turned round.

'I want to tell you something. It's about my mother. I haven't told many people this. But we're good friends now and I can trust you.'

'You can trust me. Tell me anything.'

'My mum was killed in a car crash. Her lover was

killed with her. None of us had any idea that she had a lover. Not even Dad. Until he found the love letters hidden in their room. It had been going on for five years, Carrie. In secret. That's where all my hate is, you see. That's why I do karate. I still can't accept it. I want to revenge her but I can't. How can you revenge someone who's in hell.'

'You can't mean that, Sam. Not about your own mother.'

'But the whole thing nearly destroyed my father. I just saw his heart broken and that wasn't funny.'

The kettle boiled so I made the coffee and moved a table so that we could both reach it in comfort.

'I'm sorry, Sam.' But I wondered why she had chosen that moment to tell me. You could tell she was right strung up about it.

'You see, Carrie. I need to get my act together. I've come out here to learn how to accept and how I can forgive my mother. You're important to me Carrie. I haven't got many friends. I haven't got a sister I can talk to. I mean another female. Well, I guess sometimes if you haven't got something in life then you're compensated for it in another way. I've got a lady friend. She's about forty and an author. She's the closest thing to a mother I know.'

'Does she understand?'

'She understands. So I'm lucky I guess. But for fun we've got to be sisters, Carrie, you and me. Let's pretend we're sisters. It's closer like that.'

I knew this was just Sam's way of coping with her hang-ups. This was something I had to go along with. Just for her own good. Simple as that. It's funny. First it was my problems and now it's hers. Is that what friends are for? Or is it what sisters are for?

'I've always wanted an elder sister,' I said.

'So, that's me, okay?'

'Yeah, Sam. That's you.'

'So, now that's our own secret. That's our own promise to each other no matter where we are on this earth then that secret will go with us.'

It was so important to her. I could just tell. I reached out and squeezed her hand. 'That is our secret. From now on, we're sisters.'

'You know Carrie, I'm not religious but I just wish the whole world could be like brothers and sisters. I really do.'

'That would be nice.'

'Dreams,' she suddenly smiled. 'Oh, I feel freaked. But you, Carrie. You've got some talent.'

'Oh, it's nothing. Let's quit getting deep, eh. We've got to get ready for dinner.'

'Sure, I think there's a disco on tonight or something. We'll find out from the others.'

'Okay. I'm going to have a shower.'

I was just thinking while I was under the shower. I was thinking about the world being all brothers and sisters. Well, we are I guess. We are. But no one knows it. I guess that's the trouble. No one knows it. Oh, to hell with getting deep. I just hoped Cliff wouldn't sit on the same table as us at dinner. I just hoped that.

7

We didn't see Cliff that night at dinner. We sat at a table where we discussed with the others the disco which was on that night. We heard that it was down in the cellars beneath the laundry. There was a great hall down there. They played English music and an English DJ ran it. Well everyone seemed quite excited about it. Although it was obvious some people were going just so that they could get high on more than the alcohol! That annoyed me slightly but there again I knew I would just be going to have some fun and not for any mind-blowing experience. I loved dancing anyway. Apparently it was going to be an English rock evening. All the old rock and roll numbers. Music of the sixties. Elvis. Roy Orbison, etc., etc.

Before we left the dining hall we found out that it was to start at eight and go on until one in the morning. We also had to look on the noticeboard to see which jobs we were allocated to the next day, which was Sunday. I found out that for a week I would be working in the factory. Starting at seven thirty in the morning and finishing at two which I was pleased about. It didn't seem so bad starting early when you know you'll be finished at two. It was only half the day really. Sam was on the chicken farm which she didn't moan about either, so that was okay. Anyway, we came out of the hall in a group and one of the girls, Tessa, gave me a fag which I thought was kind of her. When we split she smiled at me. We all said we'd see each other at the disco.

It took about an hour to get dressed up and put our make-up on and everything. I picked my denim jumpsuit to wear. It was like a glorified boiler suit and I always felt comfortable in it. Especially for dancing. I wear my flat cowboy boots with it and I feel really confident in the outfit. I hadn't thought about Cliff much. Not until I was applying my make-up. I did hope he'd be at the disco and that we could dance together. It didn't seem to matter about what had happened that day. It didn't matter. I just hoped he'd forgive me, that's all. Then we could both start again perhaps. We could do that.

The disco seemed to begin with a fantastic surge of energy. Fast oldies. Rock oldies. Oh, by half-past eight after we'd had our first drink inside us most of us were up on the dance floor. No one cared, you know. Or felt embarrassed. We all did our own thing and that was the most important thing. It was like everyone at the disco was crazed out on it. The atmosphere was great. It was just like everyone belonged together. Like we were all part of one body. Like a great, massive caterpillar made up of hundreds of people.

Drinking. Dancing. Rocking and rolling. All having fun. It was electric. It made my adrenalin tingle. I just loved freaking out on the dance floor. We had a table for four of us. And then Hiesha came and joined us. I looked for Cliff in the throng but I couldn't see him. I thought Hiesha was the one Sam fancied but she seemed to be chatting loads of guys up. Well, dancing with them and having them buy her drinks. Poor Hiesha, I felt rather sorry for him as she left him at the table with me. He was okay actually. I was asking him about his life on the kibbutz and he told me he had a brother and a sister. I was surprised when he told me his sister was out in the Golan Heights with the army. Not realizing that women in Israel had to do service as well. He also told me how much the kibbutz had changed since they let volunteers come here. He said he couldn't get used to life in the city because all the people moved so fast and he couldn't understand how people could live alone. Well, that was just how he was brought up. He said it made him feel insecure to do anything alone.

Yeah it was good. Anyway this tall, Dutch guy came and asked me if I wanted to dance. And seeing that Cliff still hadn't turned up I decided to accept. He was quite a good-looking guy with blonde hair and blue eyes, but I didn't think he had a patch on Cliff. But dancing with him gave me something to do before my real love came. And thinking of him I twisted round in the middle of the jive and glanced towards the door. He still hadn't turned up.

'How about me taking you out for a drink?' This guy said suddenly, which threw me off course completely.

'Christ, I wasn't expecting that.'

'Oh, do I have to learn the hard way, with you. No?' He laughed, accepting my rejection with a certain amount of grace.

The record came to an end and I must admit as I walked back to the table I felt rather dazed. I mean I had been asked out. Of that I was flattered. Perhaps I wasn't so ugly after all. But I definitely had my heart set on only one guy and he was in no way Dutch. Thinking of Cliff I looked towards the door again and that's when I saw him. My heart practically jumped in my mouth. Just to know we were so near each other. Yet again, Cliff and I. We were so near each other.

A group of people were surrounding Cliff and I

knew he loved that. He loved to be in the limelight. To be the centre of attention. He was wearing a grey, really classy suit. He really was the smartest person there. He knew it too. In fact I thought then that he may have been a bit of a poser. I knew if I was at home Zoe would have called him a poser.

'Look who's here!' Sam came over and shouted in my ear.

'Yeah, I had noticed. Are you going to dance with Hiesha?'

'Shall we go to the loo and have a chat?'

'Wait until Cliff gets here.'

'By the looks of things that could be all night.'

I just shrugged. I'd already made up my mind that I would let Sam sort out her own problems for that night. Besides she was older than me and she had more experience with the other sex. And I couldn't stop her saying yes to a dance from another of her admirers. No matter how badly I felt about Hiesha who had gone to talk to some of his Israeli friends. Anyway, I had Cliff to think about. I looked across at him and suddenly he waved at me, then he started to push his way across.

'Hello, love. You all right?' He kissed me on the cheek.

'Yeah, I'm okay. You're late.'

'Yeah, I'm looking after one of the prison kids.'

'What?'

'I'll tell you about it later. He's puking up outside at the moment. What do you want to drink?'

'Vodka and coke please.'

'I'll give it half an hour and see if he's still out there. I'll get the drinks in.'

Just watching him walk away made me go all weird inside. I couldn't explain it. I felt immensely happy.

He seemed to have forgotten all about me walking out on him. That made me want him even more. God, I felt happier than I'd felt in a long time. I really did, I'd never felt that way about any other male. Not like the way I felt then. It had just been a dream. Just a dream. That was all. I remembered the wish I'd made on blowing out my birthday cake candles that year. I'd wished for a man to come along who I'd truly love. Yes. I'd wished for an older man. Now, that wish had come true. I was in a dream. A complete and utter dream.

Sam came back then and sat down. Sweating and puffing profusely. Although she lit another fag.

'Hey!' she said. 'I've got some.' She pulled out a tiny bag and showed it to me. It was full of a white powder. I knew it was a drug in there. I didn't exactly know what drug but Sam didn't seem too worried at having it. She was laughing. I was suddenly scared.

'Sam,' I said.

'It's all right. It's free.'

'It's no laughing matter Sam. What've you got it for?'

'Don't worry. It's for someone else, not me.'

'Like, who?'

'Darling, it's sherbet, okay? You don't have to believe everything I say. You're so naïve. It's a joke pack.'

'Oh, great joke. You nearly made me have a mega heart attack, but who's to worry about that.'

'Drink on Cliff, eh?'

'Not for you,' I was slightly narked with Sam then. I mean it just made me feel really stupid when she played jokes like that. And even then I wondered if it really was drugs that she'd got hold of. I tried not to worry about it though and Sam disappeared anyway as Cliff came back.

'Thanks,' I said. But feeling slightly irked. My fault. I'm so ultra sensitive but I couldn't stop it happening.

'What's wrong pet?' He reached out and put his hand over mine which was on the table. So close, next to me. It made me think of how I'd pulled away from him. How I'd walked away from him. Like, in a way, leaving him in the lurch. I just looked down at my drink thinking, he must think I'm a moody bitch.

'Carrie?' He spoke. 'I do understand, all right?' He gently touched my chin, pushing it so that I turned to look at him. 'Carrie, I understand. No hassle, all right?'

'You're different,' I pulled my eyes from his.

'Is it impossible for you to be yourself?'

'It's not so simple to trust someone.'

'Because you haven't got a mother?'

'Because my father's a policeman and he used to be an alcoholic. For ten years he abused us. He hit me. He beat me. He dried out two years ago. He's different now but when Mum died, well, I guess I thought he was to blame. He was an alcoholic bastard. I've still got the scars to prove it.'

He said nothing. I could tell by his face that he was shocked though. After a while he spoke.

'Tell me something, Carrie.'

'What?'

'Did you paint to escape?'

'Painting was all I had. I used to get bullied at school because of Dad. Mum used to go out with black eyes. He used to bring other women home. I mean to say I have got morals, you know. If I hadn't I wouldn't have survived this long. I've got morals and I read the Bible sometimes and I paint and sometimes that's all I need. I've grown into a loner. I like being alone. I don't need anyone around me all the time. Besides, I'm difficult to please. I think I should just warn you, that's if we're going further with our relationship.'

'Is your father all right now?'

'Yeah. For two years he's been straight. He is all right now. I've forgiven him and I do love him. He did apologize. Anyway I don't usually tell my guys any of this. It's garbage. I don't know why I'm telling you really.'

'He's a policeman, isn't he?'

'Yeah, a detective. He survived at work you know. When he got home he changed.'

'Carrie. I really am sorry. But I could read the vibes you know. We won't push things. Just take it gently.'

'Sometimes I want to push things. So that somehow I'll break so that I can come up the other side. With nothing but happy memories. I have to make happy memories now. That's all,' I shrugged my words away.

'I can try to make you happy. I'd love to do it. I've got my own hang-ups, about my wife, and I can understand about alcoholics. I used to be one.'

It was my turn to be shocked. I turned away from him.

'Carrie,' he touched my head. 'Carrie, I'm like your dad. I won't be an alcoholic again. Look at what I'm drinking. Look, its apple juice. I haven't touched alcohol for five years.'

'Is that why you divorced?'

'Yes.'

'Did you used to beat your daughter?'

'Would you condemn me if I said I did.'

I stood up. 'Let's dance, Cliff. Let's dance our troubles away.'

He followed me to the dance floor and we danced.

We danced.

8

We danced. Just him and I.

'We must both promise,' he shouted over the music as we were moving our bodies in time. He was a good mover. Especially considering his age. He was showing off though, I knew that. Showing the world that he was the best. We danced and he yelled in my ear, 'We must both promise,' he repeated.

I questioned him with my eyes.

'Give up the fags. I've got high blood pressure. Doctor said I have to give up.'

'Sure,' I smiled. He looked so earnest. Me? I don't smoke that much anyway.

'We don't need it,' he yelled. But all the time trying to convince himself. 'We don't need it, Carrie. You don't need it.'

'Okay. No hassle.'

'We'll be fit.'

'Sure.'

'To move quicker on the dance floor.'

'You're nuts!' But we carried on dancing. If the truth were known I was rather showing off myself. Why shouldn't I? I was really enjoying it.

We were both whacked when we sat down again. But then we both decided, almost together, that we should go and find this prison kid that Cliff had been on about before. Just to make sure he was okay. We went out to the entrance hall and he was gone. He'd disappeared.

'Oh well,' Cliff said, 'Someone else must have picked him up.'

'Well, I don't think it was Sam.'

'One way to get you out here though, wasn't it?' He smiled and he had that kind of look in his eye. That kind of look which meant a kiss. Which meant he was thinking of us both. Physically, I mean.

'Let's walk,' he said, grabbing hold of my elbow and not giving me a chance to do anything but follow.

'Cliff?' We walked away from the hall.

'What is it, love?'

'Are you famous?'

'Quite. In the right circles.'

'But I never knew of you.'

'You obviously don't mix with the right sort of people.'

'Are you religious?'

'I believe in God the Son, God the Father and God the Holy Spirit. It's simple. Just like that. However, I'm not entirely sure where the Church is and who makes the Church work. Indeed, if my faith has anything to do with the present day Church.'

'We don't want to get into an argument about religion, but there are Satan worshippers out there, you know.'

'Yeah, they all come out on the 31st October.' He tried to laugh it off. To me, though, it was more serious. He took my hand. 'Philosophy,' he said.

I didn't answer.

'Actually,' he continued. 'Asking me if I'm religious is like me asking you if you're still a virgin.'

'Well, not quite but are you asking me now?'

'Yes. Surprise me.'

'I am still a virgin.' I didn't mind telling Cliff that, I

mean I know some girls who thought it was big to sleep around. Especially at College. But for me it had to be special. That first time. It just had to be special.

'Is that because of your religion?' he asked.

'How d'you know I'm religious?'

'I can count your vibes. I'm good at counting vibes, baby.'

'Where are we going?'

'I'm taking you through the garden to a small lake. There's a seat there and the moon and stars tonight will light up the lake.'

'And then you'll rape me, will you?'

He stopped for a minute. Just stopped and turned square to face me. Still in the dark of that moonlit night I could hear the faint sounds of the disco. About sex. Well I did trust Cliff but then if he was only after one thing. Well, it had to be hard. I've had three previous boyfriends. No sex. They wanted it. When they did, I just said: Fuck off you bastard and I never saw them again. It just couldn't be like that with Cliff, though. I didn't want to have to end it. But if he did what I suspected then what should I do?

Cliff said nothing though, just looked deep into my eyes and then we walked on a while in silence until we came to a small bank. It was like an island. It was so peaceful. We walked a bit further on and then suddenly we came to the lake. A small lake surrounded by cacti and odd sorts of plants. Cliff lead me to a log chair and we both sat down. We weren't touching or anything. I was scared a bit to be alone with him like that. But I guess it was something like walking in a time zone. Somehow I felt suddenly much older than eighteen. I felt as if I was living in a dream. Oh, if it could be like this for ever, I thought. On a continuous cloud. Just wafting and feeling lightheaded. Cliff and I. I and Cliff. That's good English. I get high too when I paint. It has to be more complicated than this. Everything has to be more complicated. It just can't be this simple.

'Carrie?'

'Yes?' I didn't avert my gaze from the reflection of the moon in the lake.

'How come you're still a virgin? You're a very pretty young woman.'

'Have you come to rape me then?'

'I want to get into your soul not your vagina.'

'That's strange, Sam said you wanted my soul.'

'You and I. We're both artists.'

'I s'pect that's why it would never work. Explain to me how you split up with your wife.'

'I became successful. I needed more and more time to do my writing. It consumed me. The only way I could get away from that pressure was to drink. So, I was knocking it back and high flying it around town. No time for my wife. No time for my daughter. I just took them all for granted. I didn't realize I loved them until it was too late. She'd had enough. I don't blame her now. It forced me to dry out. I tried to get her back but she wouldn't take the risk. I need someone now. Someone special. I need to be loved and stimulated. It's got to be natural, Carrie. When you want and when I want and it'll just come. In time. You don't have to be afraid. Its just like the moon and the stars. God's in everything. Touching everything. Like you and me. You mustn't be frightened of me. You must never be frightened of me.'

'It's the ultimate in giving yourself, isn't it? Making love. The final part of yourself.'

'You give to your partner and he gives to you. You've never had the experience before because you've never met the right man.'

'How do you know when you've met the right man, though?'

'How do you know the moon's going to shine? How do you know it hasn't suddenly lost its light? Faith. Intuition. Anything. When the time is right.'

'I need space and I need time to work. But there's still a gap only a man could fill. That silent part inside. Saying, love me. Find someone to love me. Take care of me. I can look after him and he can look after me. We can both just be one. Perhaps we can even have children. I want children, Cliff. I want them.'

'You're young to want children these days.'

'I don't really want to be an artist. I want to be a mother and a wife. That's more important to me than painting.'

'Why so strong an urge? To give up your painting.'

'In some ways it would be like getting Mum back again. I am very like my mother was, you know.'

'You really could have so much ahead of you, though.'

'I can't carry on painting, Cliff. It would be like having two lovers. That's all. I can't split myself in two. That's why the first time really has to be special. Whoever I marry I will sacrifice my gift to.'

'I couldn't do the same thing, Carrie.'

'That's because you're the professional. I'm not. It's just a hobby to me. A way to escape. I'll never be professional. I could never work that hard at it. I just couldn't see the point. All I do is dream, I never get down to the hard graft.'

'In many ways my writing always will come first. I have to fit my whole life around that. But I do know how to relax now. I don't need booze. I know I'll make a better husband the second time round.'

I said nothing. I almost felt that nothing more needed to be said. Was all this just groundwork? I wondered. Groundwork. Am I crazy, stupid even to want to be a housewife, to want to be a mother. I could dedicate my life to that. Am I stupid?

Suddenly I felt so relieved. I hadn't told anyone what I'd just told Cliff. It made me happy to have shared it with him. And suddenly he moved closer to me. I felt his arms go round me and I didn't resist. I just let him wrap himself around me and then his lips were upon mine and suddenly I felt hot. His tongue, a spear, like that because there were so many feelings inside me which I hadn't experienced before. Nothing more need to be said. And I knew then, I knew then that it would be done. One day it would be done. My first time. I knew it would be done.

9

'This is something special, isn't it?' Sam spoke to me. When we'd just finished work for the day. We'd both had our jobs changed to harvesting oranges. Not the easiest of tasks with the sun beating down on you and I'd forgotten to wear my hat so I finished up with a splitting headache. We finished work at two though and I'd just had a shower and changed into a fresh pair of shorts and a baggy tee-shirt. Sam had followed me into the shower and she was then in the process of drying her long, jet black, hair. She was getting really brown was Sam. It made her look good and I hoped my tan made me look good too. My hair was black too and long, although not as long as Sam's.

I'd just told Sam I was moving all my painting stuff over to Cliff's place. He had a small building all to himself on the kibbutz and he suggested that I do my painting in there when he was doing his writing. It was a good idea. I could paint and he could write. I guess that was something important to him. And the fact that we would be together was something important to me.

'Carrie! Are you listening to me?'

I turned to Sam.

'Are you listening?'

'Special?' As if I didn't know what she meant.

'You and Cliff. I mean, you know, is it going somewhere or what?'

'Well of course it is. I mean joking apart, we have

known each other ever since we came out here and that's near on four weeks now.'

'I know it is. I can see love in your eyes, I know. Just be careful, okay? I mean it's the first time you're been to his place.'

'You don't trust men, Sam. You don't trust them. I have to. It's a different life.'

'Well, if anything happens make sure he's wearing a condom. You don't know who he's been sleeping around with.'

I had to smile, although I was feeling a bit angry really. For Sam to put a damper on things. Just because she happens to be so cynical. I shoved my paints into a holdall and was finally ready to leave.

'Carrie?'

As I was struggling out the door. 'For God sake, I'm not five years old,' I said.

'All right.' She held up her arms in submission. 'All right. He seems an okay guy. Don't go in over your depth, though. Just that, all right?'

I loosened up a bit then. She really did seem quite perturbed about it all.

'I'll see you later, Sam. In time for dinner, okay?'

'Sure.'

I began walking over to where Cliff lived. It was in a block of white buildings where the Israelis lived. I could just about remember the way to go and I nearly got the fright of my life when someone jumped out of the bushes at me. I only calmed down when I saw that it was Cliff. He had sunglasses on and was smoking a large cigar. For a minute I went mad at him for scaring me.

'I thought you'd get lost,' he said.

'Well in that case you could have walked across for me.'

'What's the time?'

'Half past three.'

'It's Friday. Have you been working?'

'Of course I have. I don't scive off work, Cliff.'

'So, now you're not going to scive off work either. Now you're going to paint,' he grabbed hold of my easel and pad. 'By what Sam told me I'm going to convince you that you can be an artist as well as a mother. I'm used to cooking. I'm used to cleaning. I love it. Or so they say!'

'Sure. Everyone loves cooking and cleaning.'

'You undermine yourself far too much, my darling. And don't tell me I'm the professional.'

'That would be a lie wouldn't it.' I smiled.

'I just want to be a husband and a father, that's all.'

I hooted. 'Sure, so writing never comes first.'

'Well, here we are. It's a bit of a shack I'm afraid.'

It was a small white building. Rather like a bungalow. I followed Cliff down the small pathway to the door. He just opened it. There were no locks or anything. I followed him into a small hallway which lead directly into the lounge. It was quite large and brightly decorated. There was a desk in one corner with a word processor on it. There were loads of shelves brimming with books and scraps of paper seemed to be spread all across the floor.

'Well, I think there'll be room for you to work,' he said. 'Over on that side, by the window. What d'you think?'

'Yeah, there should be enough room. But hold on a minute. I thought you said you liked doing the housework!'

'It's only a mess because I've been working this morning.'

Oh yeah, I thought. A likely story.

'Anyway it adds to the atmosphere, don't you think?' he said as he began picking sheets of paper up from the floor. 'I work with music, Carrie. Would it disturb you?'

'No. I sometimes work with music too.' I was unstrapping my easel but suddenly not really feeling like painting. All I felt like doing was sitting down and dreaming that Cliff's place was my place too. That we were both married. Suddenly out of the blue, I suddenly felt a mood coming on. I stopped getting my paints out and knelt on the floor.

'What is it?' Cliff asked.

'I can't paint. I mean that. I can't do it. Not when I'm with you.'

'Why?' he frowned, completely seriously.

'I'd rather make you a cup of coffee and watch you work.'

'Carrie, I don't think you should give up. Not for me. Not for anyone.'

'Well, I'm definitely not doing any painting today,' I snapped. 'If you don't want me here I might as well go back.'

'All right. All right. You can stay. I'll make us a cup of coffee. I have been working all morning anyway. Come and I'll show you the rest of the place.'

He led me through to a small kitchen where he put the kettle on and got the cups ready for coffee. He then led the way into his bedroom. The first thing I noticed was that he had a double bed. The room was neat and tidy, it really was. It looked as if nothing was out of place. I didn't want to stick too much in the bedroom though, so, still in a mood, I turned away from him and went back into the lounge where I sat on the settee. Strangely I suddenly felt close to tears and I didn't know why. I heard Cliff in the kitchen and I hated the thought of crying in front of him. All the same when he came in with the coffees my tears were near at hand.

'You can leave your paint stuff here for another day,' he said, sitting next to me on the small settee. I was just looking at one spot. A stain on the coffee table. A stain made by a coffee mug or something.

'Carrie?'

I didn't look up, I couldn't do it. Sometimes I felt so scared. So scared of doing things which other people my age could do so automatically and without fear. Me? I was suddenly very scared. My tears were constantly, second by second, waiting to break free.

'What's wrong Carrie?'

'I'm sorry.'

'You don't have to say that, I just want to know what's bugging you and why.'

The trouble was I didn't rightfully know apart from it being because of my headache. I guess thinking so much of one person just made me feel very vulnerable. A long time ago I stopped giving myself completely to anyone. Once I'd promised not to love anyone again. No one. I learnt to be self-sufficient. That's the only way I could survive. But then, just then there was Cliff. My feelings were too strong for him. It made me scared. It made me panic in a way. It made me panic.

'Carrie, talk about it. I urge you truly to tell me.'

'Why should you want to know my secrets?'

'Are they secrets?'

'My life, that's all. Nothing to write home about.'

'Sometimes, Carrie, I mean sometimes it's like you're in a cocoon. I just can't get through. You protect yourself so well. You're so scared to come out of that protective layering. It must be like cotton wool to you. Is it nice in there, Carrie? Is it better than being out? Bad memories, Carrie. Bad memories can be released if you find someone trusting to love.'

'But can I trust you? Can I trust anyone?'

'We're friends aren't we? More than anything, we're friends. Don't cry now. You are lovable you know. I know you well, Carrie,' he wiped away a few of my tears then he smiled with a kind of twinkle in his eye. 'Carrie, I will never press you.'

'Perhaps you think everything's funny. I don't know. Anyway. I'm going. I will leave my stuff here though.'

'You're running out on me again, aren't you?'

'I guess it looks like that, yeah.'

'And we had such a good night again at the disco. You're up and down, Carrie. You're too much up and down. Learn to stabilize. For your own good.'

There was a tone of anger to his voice. I felt guilty as I started clearing my art gear. Then I picked up my fags and got ready to go. I didn't want to leave him, not if he was angry at me. But I couldn't stay. That was the truth. I just couldn't stay. So I just walked towards the door.

'Carrie,' he was up and following me out of the door. 'I'll be here all day. All evening. Waiting, OK? Waiting?' We split then. I just walked quickly away from him. Quickly away.

10

I went bombing along and stormed across the green. I knew where I was going. I knew where the water tower was and that you could get to the top of it by climbing the ladder running up its side. As I was climbing the ladder I was praying there wouldn't be anyone up top. I was lucky. There was no one. Thank God, there was no one there.

I looked out across the desert. A great layer of land in front of me. Barren. Rather mystifying. Israel. Oh yes, but it's the same, isn't it? The same as anywhere else. People are the same. People are bastards no matter where they come from.

I sat with my legs dangling over the side of the tower and then I thought of England. Of home, Dad and Zoe. I missed them then, I really did, I want to go home. I do. I hate it here. I'm out of my depth. I'm falling in love. I want to fall in love. I don't want to fall in love. Am I a prude? I'm a virgin. Does that make me a prude? Maybe I am. Oh, it's hard. Trying to analyse one's self. But then perhaps you have to, once in a while. Like getting washed out inside. England is so far away. Dad is so far away. Before I came to Israel I used to be so confident. So confident in everything. But here, well, I am just forced to wonder. I really am. Just forced to wonder.

I just happened to glance down and I saw him coming. It was Cliff. He was just wearing yellow shorts and some Jesus sandles. I waved and shouted to him. I couldn't hold back. He began to climb the ladder. Climb the ladder to be with me.

'Carrie.' When he arrived he kissed my head. 'This is your secret place, then.'

'I found it the other day. It's peaceful up here.'

'The kibbutzniks find it strange when people like to be alone.'

'They are happy with each other though, aren't they?'

'There is a war going on.'

'I know and it's too stifling sometimes.'

'It gets very tense at times. Mothers seeing their sons going to fight. Maybe their sons won't return. They are a very emotional people. It would get tense.'

'In some ways I wish I'd never come. The whole place seems too claustrophobic at times.'

'Why did you come out here?'

'I wanted to do something on my own. Make a definite break away from my family.'

'Oh, Carrie, you like to see things as black and white. In some ways you're so young. I mean some things aren't just black and white. They're mixture of greys and lights and darks.'

I looked at him. Had to listen to his words.

'Sometimes there are deep wounds. Deep.'

'I know why you're saying that.'

'Carrie, come back to my place with me. Now. Just let us relax together. Just you and me. Be brave. We can talk. We can love each other. I'm not going to let you down. Believe me!'

I looked at him. Deep into his blue eyes. For an instant I felt like a woman. A woman with feelings. Sensual feelings. But then fear came rushing back to me. I'm still a virgin. Still a virgin at eighteen. How could I be?

'Carrie?' Cliff reached to touch my hair. He ran it

through his fingers. 'Carrie, please take a chance. Do it this time.'

I smiled, felt myself blush. But why does it have to be like this? Why am I so reticent? I didn't know.

'I'm scared,' I finally said.

'How can you be scared of something beautiful?'

'You're talking about sex?'

'There is such a thing as petting you know. For God's sake, trust me, Carrie.'

'But I want you,' I turned away as I said that. 'I've never wanted anyone before. I just don't understand my own feelings, Cliff.'

His hands came about me with my back to him. He crossed his arms about my breasts. Oh God, I felt so weird. I couldn't keep pushing him away. And why should I anyway? Really, why should I?

'Your feelings are natural. Don't run from them. Go with them,' he spoke in my ear. Oh God, it was so good. To be so close to him and I could feel everything in my heart fading. Really fading. All my fears. All my previous hang-ups. On God, I bent my head down and bit on his arm. Just bit on it. His taste. His love. His presence. I let him turn me around. He cupped my face in his hands. And they were so strong. I didn't want it to stop. Not that moment when we were so close. So very close. I pulled his thumb into my mouth.

'Oh, Carrie. You're so good. You really are. We'll go back to my place and I'll cook some tea for us, okay?'

I didn't object. I didn't need to object. Suddenly my heart was going. Suddenly I felt the whole damn thing with Cliff was right. I needed and wanted him so much. How could I leave him again. How could I run out on him. It suddenly felt like I would always have him. For ever and ever and that's what I wanted. I wanted to be with him forever.

We went back to his place. I let him lead me. I was still a bit worried but then I let my feelings take over. After all, I am a women. I am the same as everyone else. I can't hide from that. And I sat on the couch in Cliff's place and I let him bring his arms around me.

When he took my bra off I felt odd. Just slightly. Well, it was the first time anyone had got that far with me. But everything then had been leading up to that with Cliff. I knew what he wanted when he led me back to his place. I knew I wouldn't run. I knew something would happen. I felt so inexperienced. I unbuttoned his shirt and kept thinking I was doing the wrong thing. He had a mass of hairs on his chest and his stomach. I let my hands wander over his body, just as my bra came away. God, I didn't think anything could feel this good. I really didn't. He gently eased me down on the sofa until I was lying. Then he unzipped my jeans.

It all happened. But then it didn't all happen. We didn't actually make love that time. Somehow I got the impression that Cliff didn't want to. We went so far though and I felt so good, so mature, so elated. I looked at Cliff as he put his pants and shorts on again and his shirt. I was just lying there naked, puffing on a fag. Taking it all in. Trying to relive the experience, which I knew I would. When I went back to my shack I knew I'd be dreaming about it.

'Let me finish off your fag. Put your clothes on, eh? I'll go and put the kettle on.'

'Okay. What's the time?'

'About three.'

'It's gone so quickly. I feel spaced out.'

'Hey, come on.' He pointed a finger at me. 'Get dressed.'

'Haven't you got a dressing gown I could put on. For now?'

'Don't be so lazy, girl. I said get changed?'

'Oh, you're bossy. Have you got another girlfriend or something going to come?'

'No, but if you don't put some clothes on pretty soon I'm going to be overcome by passion and at the moment I'm trying to restrain myself, okay?' He smiled at me. Then he slapped me on the leg. 'So, I'll put the kettle on and you get changed.'

'Give me one more kiss and I will.'

'For Christ sake!! You're acting just like a bloody teaser. It's you who doesn't want to go the whole way.' Because he really did sound a bit angry then I just poked my tongue out at him and let him go out to the kitchen. As much as I didn't want to I got up and began putting my clothes on again.

Cliff made a pot of tea and some sandwiches which he filled with this cream cheese stuff which was really nice. It was sort of fluffy and Cliff said most people mix it with jam but he'd ran out. Anyway we chatted about this and that as we were having our tea then I remembered to ask him something which I'd been meaning to ever since the disco and the prison boy he'd been looking out for.

'Cliff, why did you call that boy a prison boy? You know at the first disco. He was drunk or something.'

'Oh, yeah, Rehan you mean.'

'I didn't know his name.'

'You've seen them around though, haven't you? Around the kibbutz. We call them the prison kids.'

'Yeah, I know you do, why?'

'They're only on the kibbutz because they've been sent here by the Courts. If they weren't here they'd be in a remand place or some of the older ones like Rehan would be in prison. They've all done something wrong. You know, stealing, fighting. Stuff like that. Sending them to live on the kibbutz is like they're giving them a final chance to sort themselves out. Like an alternative to prison, you know?'

'How many of them are there?'

'About fifteen. This guy called Shanan is in charge of them. He's a mate of mine. A good bloke. Sometimes he gets me to look out for them at the disco. You know, just in case. Yeah. God, Shanan's a hard man though. He's harder than them kids. That's why he's doing a good job. Because they're all scared of him. And because of that he gets their respect. Which really, is what it's all about.'

It was interesting. Hearing all about the prison kids. I had seen teenagers about. Israeli boys and girls. And they had seemed a bit rough but I hadn't known any of what Cliff had told me. Actually I rather hoped Cliff would introduce me to Shanan. I could ask him quite a few questions. Like, what are the prisons like in Israel and what are the main problems for the young ones. I was interested in anything like that. A bit of intrigue and all.

Anyway after we'd had our tea Cliff told me he wanted to do some writing. He said I'd inspired him, As it was seven o'clock by that time I wasn't really worried and thought I could spend some time with Sam instead. Down the bar, perhaps. Cliff and I spent about fifteen minutes on a lingering goodbye and then I left him. For the second time that day. But this time I was happy. I wasn't storming off in a mood or anything. I was more than definitely OK.

11

That time with Cliff was the first of many afternoons and evenings that we spent together. I used to go round there at about three and stay until late. In a way we had a routine going. He'd cook the tea, usually something on toast. Then we'd watch telly while eating. Then we'd do a bit of tidying and put music on. I painted sometimes and he wrote but more often than not we were just loving each other. Exploring. Finding out what we both liked. He didn't push me. Not on the final act. But everything Cliff and I did was building up to the climax. And that's what I wanted and shared in. The foreplay. The games. The love and it was so flexible. It was so undemanding. We were so right for each other. Day after day we'd spend together. I was just so besotted. There was time for work and that was all practically. I saw Sam. I was still sharing a room with her and we were mates but she'd made her own friends which made me feel less guilty at me spending such a lot of time with Cliff. But suddenly it seemed that my whole life was changing and it made me feel good. Really damn good. It wasn't only the physical side of our relationship which was good though. Cliff told me I stimulated him because I was intelligent. I was mature for my age. But he said being mature didn't make me into a tart. I mean he said he knew he could trust me. And it was the same with me really. Cliff really was so brilliant. Creative and interested in everything which was going on in the world. We would spend hours having in depth conversations about things. Reading books on the history of Israel together and other countries which Cliff had been to. You see all in all we had a proper rounded relationship. We just inspired each other so much and I'd never felt that way before. Never in my whole life about a man. I really hadn't.

I was surprised when Cliff bought me the ring. One evening he put it on my finger. He said it was an engagement ring but that was the first we'd spoken about getting engaged. He'd been in Haifa for the day with his mates. He actually admitted to me that he'd been drinking. It did worry me a bit but then I thought he didn't get drunk. I mean everyone drinks a bit. Cliff could be no different from any normal man. When he gave me the ring it sort of put my mind at rest about him drinking. He'd probably changed just as much as I had during the past few weeks.

'Carrie, now we're engaged I think the time's probably right to ask you.'

I was sitting on his lap and I turned to face him. Pushing some hair back from his forehead.

'Well I think now, I mean now it's time that you came and lived with me. Here. Just us two. You know? I mean we have known each other for three months now. It would just be the natural road for our relationship.'

I frowned. 'Are you drunk?'

'I swear I'm not drunk. It's just important that we're both together, that's all. At this time. You and me.'

'Oh, Cliff,' I kissed him on the cheek. 'I want to come and live with you, I do. But if we're engaged.

Well, I don't know. It's come as a shock. You know?'

'It's not a shock that I love you. I need you here. I want to make love to you. You will won't you? I mean, the time's right.'

I nodded. Because he was right. It was time. I'd been waiting for it actually. We practically knew everything about each other's body. I had no more hang-ups about sex. I was prepared to give myself completely to Cliff.

'Carrie, will you please come and live here?'

I nodded. Suddenly thinking how good it would be to actually live with him. I mean it would hardly be any different really. I practically spent all my waking hours in his place anyway. But just to make people see how serious we were about each other.

'Does that mean yes?'

'Yes, Cliff. Yes.'

As I walked back to our shack I clenched my fists in glee. I was dying to tell Sam. And to show her my engagement ring which was a blue sapphire with diamonds all around it. I felt so happy and knew I'd be writing to Zoe to tell her. Well she'd always wanted me to find a brother for her. Now, it just looks as if I have. It really does.

'For Christ sake, he's forty! Carrie, listen to me. He hasn't fallen in love with you. How can you fall in love after knowing someone for a few months? Do you know he's an alcoholic?'

I looked at her, frowning.

'He only wanted to get engaged because he'd been on a drinking binge. Look, Carrie. I feel responsible for you. That's all.'

'I'm not listening to you, Sam. You're just jealous.'

'What's changed your mind anyway? I thought

your virginity wasn't up for grabs. How do you know how many girls he's bedded since living here? That's all he wants you for.'

'You were telling me. You were telling me he's after my soul. Not my body. Now you're telling me something completely different.'

'Oh, Christ,' Sam sighed. She flopped down on her bed. 'There's no harm in having sex with him, but actually to live with him! Talking about marriage and all that crap.'

'I just know he's the right one.'

'It could just be infatuation on your part.'

'And it could be that I love him and he loves me.'

'Okay. Okay. Forget it. See what you think of him after living with him for a few weeks. I tell you, in three weeks you'll regret ever having gone with him.'

'Well, you never have liked him much since we met him. At least he doesn't take drugs.'

'You're so naïve, girl. You really are.'

'I love Cliff. I can make my own decisions.'

'Well, make sure he's wearing a condom. You don't want to catch Aids as well as everything else.'

'Sam?'

She looked at me.

'I'll make sure he's wearing a thousand condoms if you'll still be my friend.' I wasn't really angry at Sam putting Cliff down. I knew she had been shocked by my decision. At the actual fact that as long as the kibbutz committee agreed then that would be final. I guess Sam was just upset at seeing me go. We'd both come to rely on each other quite a bit since living together. Now a guy has come along and taken me away from her. Something like that, I guess. I had to convince Sam, I really had to convince her that I'd still be around and we could still be friends together.

Sam said nothing. She was just staring at the ceiling.

'Sam?'

'We remain friends,' she spoke absent-mindedly. Still gazing at the ceiling.

'Well, is that what you want?'

'I lost my virginity when I was fifteen. I envy you yours. I don't want it to be spoilt by the wrong guy.'

'The reckless side of me wants to try.'

'Well, you've certainly changed since we've been here.'

'I always said I wanted a husband and children.'

She looked at me then. Kind of seeming less put out then. As if she was accepting the news in a better frame of mind.

'I guess you'd better pack your bags then. Anyway if you can drag yourself away from Cliff perhaps we'll still get to meet up someday. I'll see yer. I'm going for a run.'

I let her go. Suddenly feeling guilty about the whole thing of moving out. Sam had made me feel like that. Oh well, life can be difficult at times. I guess one has to try and treat it like an adventure. Perhaps a circus act. Now, am I on the tightrope or am I on the tightrope?

'To hell with it,' I spoke aloud. This is it. This is me going places. Growing. Becoming a true woman. I started packing. I was in the middle of it when Don came in. He told me that the kibbutz people didn't mind me living with Cliff but I'd still have to work. Actually, Don was really great about it. He lived near Cliff with his girlfriend so, I guess, he could understand.

'Carrie, just one thing,' he said as he was on his way out, 'Well, d'you think you can handle it?'

'What?'

'He is much older than you.'

'That's okay. I can treat him like a sugar daddy.'

'He is a good man, though. I haven't seen his heart turned towards anyone since he's been here. And that's about six months now.'

I couldn't help but smile. After all that pessimistic garbage Sam had turned out on me. It was nice hearing compliments about Cliff.

'Don't forget, if you've got any hassle you can always talk to me privately.'

'Thanks, Don, I'll remember that.'

'Good luck, then,' he winked at me before he went and once again I felt elated. I really felt elated. I kept singing as I was packing. Singing: 'I'm getting married in the morning. I'm getting married in the morning.' It was something, you know. It really was something.

I carried all my stuff out of the hut which had been my home. Now, I was on the move. In fact, I felt quite important as I walked past all the volunteer's huts. Lots of them were sprawled on the grass, sunbathing and listening to their radios. A group of them asked me where I was going and I told them the truth. Proud to tell them. That'll give them something to stab me in the back for, I thought. Not giving a shit, really. Not giving a shit what they thought or said.

'Oh, we can come round, then,' one of the girls said. 'We can come and watch the telly.' I just smiled and carried on walking. Huh! They wouldn't get within two yards of Cliff's front door. Not if I had anything to do with it anyway. The unsociable brat that I was. And not even that could make me nervous about going to Cliff's. It was right, that's all I knew. It was right for both of us.

It really was a new life moving in with Cliff. The most important thing was that he didn't push himself on me, mentally or physically. Although we slept in the same bed we hadn't yet made love. He just made me feel so comfortable and relaxed in bed. Touched places which hadn't been touched before. It was like a crazy stimulant. Just gently. So gently. And his love, his strong and powerful love which always came through.

One evening we were sitting on the couch next to each other. Cliff had just put on a record. It was a romantic one. A compilation of romantic hits. That was a sign and I must have known it. I just had the feeling that the evening would be something special. Something different. I had that feeling. He poured us a glass of wine each and then touched my glass with his.

'To the artist from the author,' he said.

'Are you all right?' Because he suddenly looked a bit far away. A bit out of sorts.

'I'm just thinking. Thinking of you and it scares me. I guess I've been thinking a lot of you just lately. Always on my mind. Like the song goes. Always on my mind. Are you offended?'

'Of course I'm not. I think of you too. Quite a bit.'

'Aah, when you're on top of the cooling tower.'

'Maybe. Yes.'

'I've spied you up there, haven't I? Just contemplating. A fair lady. A very beautiful woman just contemplating. You are a woman, Carrie. There is no doubt about that. You're a very beautiful woman too.'

I looked down at my hands. I didn't know how to react.

'I want to ask you something, Carrie. But I really don't want to offend you.'

'I won't be offended.' I looked into his blue eyes. The depth in them was amazing. They comforted me.

The depth and understanding. They always have comforted me.

'It is right that you've never made love to a man before?'

'That's right.' I wasn't offended. I knew that evening was going to be special all along. I knew it. 'No, I guess I'm still a virgin.'

'Because you want to be?'

'Because I've never felt that way about a man before.'

'Me?' He almost said that in a whisper. A look of pain in is eyes. A slight look of pain.

I spoke but it was like I couldn't recognize my own voice. It seemed not to belong to me. It seemed to belong to someone much older. Someone much more mature. 'I would like you,' I said. 'I mean, I would like to make love to you. I fancy you. I would like to make love to you. I'd like you to be the first one. That would be special to me.'

He suddenly put his glass down and wrapped his arms around me. I put my drink down too and cuddled up against him. Oh, it felt so good. It really did feel so good. I don't know why I started crying. I did though. I'd never felt that warm before, you see. I'd never felt that strong feeling of being loved.

After a while, Cliff gently lifted my face to his. 'Tears?' He said.

'I'm sorry.'

'No, you don't have to be sorry. This is a special moment for both of us.'

'I love you Cliff. I do.'

'Oh Carrie, I want you so much. I need you. My body pines for you. I don't want you to go. I don't want you to ever be apart from me. My wife, I loved. I haven't loved anyone since our divorce. You must believe me.'

'I do believe you. I do. I feel so good. That's why I'm crying. I always cry when I'm happy.

'I'm forty and you're eighteen.'

'I don't care about anything apart from you. Oh, I wish we were in England.' I pulled away from him. 'It all seems so unreal out here. So far-fetched.'

'Like a dream, I know. Just like one of your paintings. You've got great talent, Carrie. You will get there.'

'I want to get there with you.'

'Life must go on with us both.'

'Do you still love your ex-wife?'

'No, I love you. I love you, Carrie.' He took a chunk of my hair in his hand and he kissed it. 'Will you make love to me, Carrie? Tonight? Can we come together? Can this be our special night?'

'Of course. Yes. As long as you use something. I'm not on the pill and what with Aids and everything.'

'I'd never hurt you, Carrie. You mustn't be afraid. I'll wear a condom.'

I smiled. I smiled in acknowledgement. It was the right time, I thought. It really was the right place and time.

He didn't hurt me. It was the most wonderful experience of my whole life. He was so gentle. So caring. So compassionate. He took me in his bed and I reached heights I'd never reached before. Heights like the heights of the Israeli mountains. Like that and more.

I was so happy. As we were lying back in bed smoking fags, I felt so gloriously, gloriously happy. It was pure ecstasy. It really was.

'Christ!' Cliff suddenly half yelled.

'What?'

'It split. The condom split, didn't it.'

I was so overwhelmed with joy that it didn't really register with me. Cliff seemed concerned at first but I talked him out of it.

'I won't get pregnant,' I said and I was sure of it. 'Not all of it got through anyway, did it?'

'Most of it did.'

'Don't worry about it, Cliff. I'll be all right.'

'I'll make sure you're all right, whatever happens. Anyway, I'm sure you won't fall. Not like this. Really.'

'Don't worry, Cliff. This night has been the most wonderful of my whole life. It really has. Nothing can spoil that. Nothing can. Our special night. And I'm not a virgin any more. I'm not a virgin any more.' I brought my lips to his and we kissed. Long and lingering we kissed with our naked bodies wrapped around each other. With our naked bodies wrapped around each other, we kissed.

12

I told Sam. I told Sam as we set off to walk across the desert the next day. I told her what had happened the previous night. Then I told her about the accident. She was shocked. To say the least she was shocked.

'Oh, don't worry. I'm hardly likely to get pregnant.'

'Yeah, but Carrie, there is a chance. You've got to know, there is a chance.'

'Well, I'm due in two weeks so I'll soon know.'

'Don't sound so glib about it. It's a serious matter.'

I did feel slightly glib about it, though. I could hardly imagine the thought of me being pregnant. I was just thinking for the next week, I was thinking, well as soon as I start. As soon as I start my period it will put Sam's fears at rest. In fact, it would prove her wrong. I felt slightly niggled with Sam, actually. She was so down to earth sometimes I couldn't imagine what made her like that. She was also much quieter just lately. She seemed to spend most of her time alone. I only put it partly down to the fact that Hiesha had gone off to war. She was very upset at him leaving. I know. But she still had so many friends on the kibbutz, boys as well as girls, so I thought she would have got over it okay. When I tried to ask what was bugging her she just said she was fed up with the place. I did feel a bit guilty at first. Because I had left her in the lurch slightly. But then a Danish girl had moved into her hut and I thought that would have made Sam happier, but it didn't seem to. Anyway, I tried to redeem my guilt by realizing I wasn't responsible for her life or happiness. Not all the time anyway. Besides at the time I had too much to think about myself. What with Cliff and adjusting to living with him. And then with the risk of pregnancy looming in the background.

I guess both Cliff and I were worried first of all about the fact that I could be pregnant but as my period wasn't due until fourteen days time we seemed to stop worrying about it for a time. Indeed, it was like the peace before a storm. We made love again, three times. The condom stayed intact each time. We were happy. Both of us were. Our lovemaking was so much fun. Fun and we both tried to make it original. Cliff had a large book about sex and we used to pore over that and try some of its ideas out. So that was the peace we had. Pushing our worries to the back of the shelf. Where they belonged, I thought. Where they truly belonged. It wasn't until I happened to tell Cliff that I was due in four days that he began to change. Began to get more anxious and alert about the whole thing.

I didn't worry too much when I was a day late in starting my period. I usually didn't start until I was two days overdue. So, I wasn't really concerned then. However, when I was a week late and I still hadn't started I must admit to worrying just a bit.

'Have you?' Cliff asked when I came out of the bathroom that morning. That had been his question for the past week, when I appeared from the bathroom each morning.

I shook my head. He looked worried but I felt the same by that time. I sat down and took the cup of coffee he gave me.

'I can't be pregnant,' I said.

'You haven't been sick, have you?'

'Actually, I have. It could just be this bug going around, though. I was sick this morning but it doesn't mean anything.'

'Of course it means something,' he suddenly yelled.

'Well, don't get stroppy. I can't do anything about it.'

'Make an appointment with the doctor. Have a test.'

'All right. I'll arrange it with Don, today.'

The test was all booked up and I just had to wait two days for the result and that was a hard two days. Cliff seemed to always be out. It seemed he couldn't bear being in the same place as me. I thought it was just the pressure. It was. Perhaps he couldn't take too much responsibility or something. Maybe I began to wonder then. Maybe, as I waited for the test. Maybe then I had a few doubts. Just seeds sown in my mind about Cliff. I just thought he could have been more supportive. Instead he just wanted to run. Me? I wanted to be pregnant and I didn't want to be. What the hell. I tried not to think about it. As the test grew nearer then I had to try and relax. Trying to convince myself that if I was pregnant, Cliff and I would get married and everything would be okay. Well, I always have been optimistic.

'For Christ sake, Cliff. That's the answer. I'm pregnant. I'm pregnant with your child.' I stood there yelling at him. Half in panic myself. Wanting him to be strong. To support me.

'God, no, it's not possible,' he half wailed, swinging away from me.

'The fact is I'm pregnant, Cliff. It's very much possible. But surely, we are going to get married anyway. That was our plan wasn't it?'

'We don't want a child, Carrie. I mean you, you can't have a child.'

'Why not? You keep telling me what a woman I am.'

'Maybe we would have got married. We wouldn't have had a child though. No, not for about two or three years. I can't look after a baby, I could never do it. My ex-wife was so strong. But she wasn't an artist.'

I suddenly felt completely and utterly confused. I mean, what the hell was happening? I was shocked about being pregnant. But it wasn't the end of the world for Cliff and I. No, I was pleased in some ways. It had been one of my dreams to become pregnant. Of falling in love with someone like Cliff. Of having a white wedding. It had been one of my dreams. But now? Now, I could see the panic in Cliff's eyes. I could see the fear. He had almost gone a deathly white.

'Cliff!'

He was pacing the room. He lit a fag, nervously puffed on it. God, it was like someone close to him had just fallen down dead in front of him.

'We'll have to do something,' he muttered. 'I know who you can go to. I'll pay for it.'

'What d'you mean?'

'I mean abortion. That's our only hope now.'

I couldn't believe it. I really couldn't believe what was happening. I was shocked, but with Cliff's words sprung at me I felt a certain amount of anger too. Anger and disgust. Disgust at what he was saying.

'Abortion!' I half screamed. 'What the hell are you

talking about? I've got a life inside me. A human life. Are you telling me? Are you telling me you want our baby aborted?'

'It's not our baby, can't you see? It was a mistake. It was just a mistake.'

'I won't have it aborted. Maybe it was a mistake but doesn't a life mean anything to you?'

'It's not like a baby. Not yet. It will be easily aborted. I know an excellent doctor.'

'Oh yeah! Does he abort all your mistakes then?' I was fuming then. Fuming, but half on the verge of tears too. I had to shout and scream. I had to. Just to get in control of my feelings. All my emotions. 'Cliff, we're unofficially engaged. You gave me this ring three weeks ago. What finger is it on, Cliff?'

'For God's sake, it's only a ring I bought you. I didn't pledge my whole life away. And I definitely didn't propose to bring our child into the world. I'm not ready for it. I'm really not.'

'I don't believe this,' I was shadowing him; step by step. 'Are you telling me this ring means nothing? Can't you see?' I held it up to him. Jabbing it in the air to make my point. 'Are you now saying it's worthless? Emotionally worthless! Oh yeah, now comes the testing time. Christ, you've got to laugh haven't you? You really took me in, Cliff. You had me lapping at your feet. For God's sake, you don't love me. You don't love me, do you Cliff? How can you love me when you don't even know what love is? You're just a slimy, fucking, bastard.'

'There's been a dreadful mistake,' he whimpered. His face creasing up. 'I've got to go out.' He grabbed his jacket and fled. Something like a scalded cat. He ran out on the problem. I knew what he was doing. I watched him do it. He was a runner. And that's when it sunk home to me. He was nothing but a feeble, weak, emotional runner. It was all show. All for sentimentality. There was nothing else to it. Nothing at all.

I flopped down on the couch and my tears came. It wasn't because I was pregnant but it was because I knew I'd lost Cliff. We were too high. Through my tears I realized that. It was just like a holiday romance. Cliff wasn't the one to take on responsibilities. He just couldn't handle it. I cried. Yes, I cried. It had all seemed so wonderful. Really, it had all seemed so brilliant. But good things have to end. I knew it was over then. I really knew that. It's over. Knowing it, I now have to try and accept it. Accept my pregnancy. Accept losing Cliff. I had to do that to the best of my ability. Truly, to the best of my ability.

13

I packed my rucksack and then went to find Don. I didn't tell him I was pregnant but told him I'd be moving out of Cliff's place.

'Want to talk?' he offered.

'I'll tell you when I'm ready, all right?'

'Bema, the Danish girl has moved on. You can go in with Sam if you like. Cheer her up a bit, eh?'

I smiled, 'I'll take my stuff in then.'

'I am sorry, Carrie. If it hasn't worked out.'

'Oh well.' I tried to bite back on the tears. 'It's no one's fault. Not really.' And then I got out of the office quick so that I wouldn't dissolve into a sobbing wreck.

It was hard. It was like being without a vital part of your body. As crucial as your lungs perhaps. That crucial. I just walked, head down. Hands in pockets. Away from him. Away from him. I've got a baby, I kept thinking. And I really couldn't believe that I was pregnant. I'm carrying an illegitimate child. And then I remembered, I remembered about my own mother. She had been illegitimate too. How odd. What coincidence. Life. Going round in circles. If you're not careful you just wind up where you started from. Huh! Where the hell did I start from? The moment I had seen Cliff, I had felt I knew him. I just knew a part of him which had to be mine. Like capturing a beautiful butterfly. My dreams. Where are they now? Where is he now? Where is he when I need him to be a father to our child. A child in my very womb. What is it, child? Will you stir inside my womb and know? Will you?

I sat on my old bed in Sam's room and absolutely bawled. It was such a great sense of loss. This is the time. This is the time when you feel a loss. When you're all alone. In a far off country. When you realize what a stupid and naïve eighteen year old you've been.

Sam came dashing in. She looked as white as a ghost.

'It's not true,' she half yelled in my ear and I could have wondered at her concern. 'For Christ sake, answer me! I've just seen Cliff. It's not true, is it?'

'You mean, am I pregnant? Is that what he told you? I guess it'll soon be round the whole bloody kibbutz. But anyway, who cares? What the hell. Yes, I'm pregnant. I really am pregnant.'

'Why have you walked out on Cliff, then?'

'Don't scream!'

'I'm not. I'm not. I'm just asking. He is the father.'

'He wants me to have an abortion. I'm not killing my baby.'

'No one's forcing you to, are they? But what the hell are you going to do? You've got to discuss it with Cliff.'

'Cliff is nothing, Sam. He really is nothing. Just a dream, that's all. I wouldn't have him back now. Not even if he came begging.'

'He was just shocked but he loves you, Carrie. I know he does.'

'He loves me this much.' I twisted the ring from my finger and threw it across the room. 'Bollocks to Cliff, that's what I say. I'm going back to England, Sam. I've got to discuss things with my family.'

'All right. I'll come with you. I'm sick of this place.'

I blew my nose and looked at her. 'What's happened, Sam? Why the hell did we come out here? For Christ sake, I'm pregnant. I've got myself a baby.'

'And a husband?'

'I guess it's up to him. If he comes back to England. I'll leave it entirely up to him. The ball's in his court so to speak. I won't go running to him, though. Not for anything will I go running to him.'

'Maybe I don't blame you, Carrie. He's a crazy kind of a guy, really. Strung up. I guess most writers are.'

'Aren't you really happy here, Sam?'

'No. Not really. I feel stifled by the atmosphere. Anyway, I guess I've half made my mind up – as to what I want to do for the rest of my life or thereabouts.'

'You mean, a career?'

'Yeah,' she looked far away.

'What?'

'I want to try and get into the policeforce.'

I had to smile. I really had to smile.

'I thought you'd laugh,' she said.

'It's only because of my dad, you know.'

'Yeah, I thought that.'

'Actually, I think you'd make a good policewoman.'

'Maybe then I'll go into plain clothes.'

'Sure you will, I know.'

'Oh, Carrie, what the hell are you going to do? You do love Cliff, don't you? All feelings can't just suddenly vanish. You'll have to stick in there if you want him badly enough.'

'It was infatuation. I knew when he reacted the way he did about me being pregnant. I knew then, deep inside. He doesn't want the hassle. Not of a baby. So, there's no point, is there? There really is no point.'

'You're a brave person to go it alone.'

'I'll have my dad and my sister.'

'How is your dad going to take it?'

'I'm going up the cooling tower, okay? Just to think. If Cliff does come, you know where I'll be.'

'Okay. I'll let him know if he comes.'

I'd been sitting there for practically an hour, in the fading sunshine, when I heard Cliff's voice. I looked down and he was halfway up the ladder.

'Carrie?' He just stood there. Such pain in those eyes of his. Such pain. I couldn't stop my heart from giving out to him. From wanting him again. From wanting him to hold me tight. I didn't go to him, though, and he didn't come to me. We both kept our distance.

'You've given me your address in England,' he started. 'In two days time I'm going to Greece. I've got some friends out there. After that, I'll come back to England for a while. I can see you then, can I?'

My whole soul seemed to sink to my feet. This was it. This was it. The ultimate. The goodbye. The good luck kiss. Goodbye. I won't see you again but good luck. A kiss to go on your way. Betrayed. I really felt betrayed then.

'Carrie, I will see you then. I promise.'

But somehow that was an empty promise. Empty as my empty heart. Hollow. All dug out.

'Do you care?' I spoke. A voice which seemed to echo in from the desert. 'Do you really care for anyone? Or are you too scared to take a risk? I'm having your baby, Cliff. It will be your flesh and blood. Don't come and see me in England. We don't need you. Not my baby. Not me. You're just a deceiver, that's all you are. A patronizing, conceited deceiver. I guess I had to learn, Cliff. Well, I will learn something from this. At least I've got a baby now. My dream come true. I just hope it doesn't turn out like you.'

'But, Carrie, you could come out to Greece too. After you've had the baby. My friends and I share a villa together. We could both go out there. Then we could get a nanny to look after the baby.'

'Christ! I don't believe this.'

'It's true. That's what we could do.'

'Cliff, don't you see? We're in different worlds. I don't belong in your world. You went to private school. Boarding school. Oh, what's the fucking point. Your condom split. God Cliff, you're the pits. Just forget it, okay?'

'That is my only offer.'

'Yeah, I guess it must be. An offer you damn well knew I'd refuse. Don't worry, Cliff. I don't need anything from you. Not your money. Not your being. Not your pigging heart. I'll see you around. Maybe.' I just walked away from him then, to climb down. I felt bad but happier at letting off some of my anger. It made me feel less tense. All I could think of then was getting back to England. It really was. I couldn't wait. I really couldn't wait.

14

Don took Sam and I into Tel Aviv the next day to sort out our air tickets and to book our flight. We arranged for us to fly back in exactly two days time. Suddenly I felt happier. Well, so did Sam. Knowing we would be out of it. Out of it in such a short time.

'Well?' She turned to me when we came out of the agency with our tickets.

'That's settled.'

'It's a weight off my mind. I want to go home, Carrie. I really do. To get on with life. In a way me coming out here was like running away. Sort of. Well, I have to get on with my life now. I'm ready to do that.'

'Well, I guess there's been a purpose for us both, coming out here. Now we're going home. I'm glad. I am really glad.'

'God, I admire you, Carrie. If it was me who was pregnant I'd be cracking up.'

'Maybe that's because you don't really want a child.'

'Oh perhaps one day. Perhaps,' she smiled at me and wrapped her arm around my shoulders. 'I'll be your child's godmother,' she said. 'I promise.'

'You can be,' I saw tears in Sam's eyes and I sort of had tears in my eyes. It was so hard, thinking of leaving the life we barely knew. But Sam and I had stuck together. We'd stuck together and we knew we'd always be friends. We really would. Considering I had few friends in my life that was quite something for me.

Anyway, Don told us that as we had been such good

workers on the kibbutz we could have our last two days completely to ourselves. It was good. All the day before our flight we spent by the swimming pool. It was easy. Just to think I'm pregnant, and I guess I sort of felt happier about that as well. It was like something special. Knowing there was another being, another being growing inside of me. A being that belonged to me. Who would have to depend on me. Someone who would love me and look up to me. Well, I've never been in that position.

'We're going home,' Sam kept saying. She wouldn't stop about us going home. 'I've missed my old man, you know,' she said. 'Even my brother and I've hated him enough in the past. I really have.'

I just lay in the sun hearing her prattle on. Only occasionally I thought of Cliff. When I did there was pain there. There was heartache but then I knew I had to cope. Not just for my own sake but for the baby as well. My baby. Our baby? Well, perhaps.

'You're not under any illusion, are you?' Sam turned on her side to approach me directly with that question.

I frowned.

'You don't actually think that Cliff will be there for you? In England. You know, you're not secretly dreaming, are you?'

'Sometimes I dream. But I know the truth. I know the truth. It hurts, Sam. It hurts but we all have to come through pain sometimes. All of us do.'

'You'll feel better at home,' she said, winking at me.

'Sure. There's always hope.' I smiled.

In someways it was hard on our last morning at the kibbutz. The word had somehow got round about me being pregnant, but, strangely enough it rather endeared me to people. They seemed sympathetic and understanding. In a way, I suddenly realized I had made quite a few friends on the kibbutz.

Don was driving us both to Ben Gurioun airport. He was borrowing the kibbutz mini-bus. On the morning of departure he helped us clear all our luggage and load it aboard the bus. Quite a large group of people were watching and waiting for us to go. I suddenly felt quite a celebrity.

I had rang Dad after we'd arranged the flight. I'd told him what time we'd be arriving at Gatwick and he said he'd be there. So, I just hoped he'd keep to his word. I hadn't told him I was pregnant, not over the phone, so that would have to wait its proper turn. Sam had also rang home and her brother was picking her up. Taking her home to Sussex, where she lived. I was dreading the thought of saying goodbye to Sam. I hoped it wouldn't be too emotional. But then I never have been one for controlling myself at goodbyes.

In a way it was strange when we finally got on the plane. We had been excited all that morning with the goodbyes and with the thought of going home but then when we were actually on the plane, on our way to England, we were suddenly rather subdued. In a way it was like an anti-climax once the next stop was England. I felt a bit down you know and then I got to thinking of Cliff and the fact that I hadn't said goodbye to him. Oh God. He had my address though. But then thinking of Cliff made me think of reality again. I'm pregnant, that reality. I've got a baby. Who knows, that reality is stark enough. Stark enough for anyone. The thought of telling Dad made me feel quite sick. How the hell he would react, I just couldn't imagine.

I allowed myself to hope. Just to remain a bit cheerful. Hope that Cliff and I would somehow come through. Come through it together. That made me happy at being pregnant. It had to. I was glad I was having a baby. But what the hell's the point of worrying? You just have to take each day as it comes. In a way I was living in a complete dream anyway. I suddenly thought that we'd land in England and I wouldn't be pregnant any more. That I'd been unconscious in a hospital in England. Just dreaming we'd been to Israel. Just dreaming that I'd met Cliff. If there was an opt out to my situation it was just me imagining such a thing. I tried to tell myself that I would have to face the problem squarely. It just made my stomach ache to think of telling Dad. It really did.

'Thinking of getting home?' Sam said, and I could tell by her eyes that she knew what I was worrying about. I just nodded.

'Don't worry,' she touched my arm.

'Would you worry about telling your dad?'

'Your old man seems pretty flexible to me.'

'It's just like the whole thing in Israel was just a dream. Now, we're just getting back to reality. It's scary. Thinking about the whole thing.'

'It's only natural to be a bit shell-shocked. Your dad will understand. I just have a gut feeling that he will.'

'It's not just that but the age gap between me and Cliff.'

'I knew you were hoping about him. He'll come to England. He'll find you. He'll want to be with you and the baby. Well? You are hoping?'

'Do you think I'm wrong to hope?'

'Well, you still love him, don't you?'

I shrugged. 'I don't know what I'll feel like when I'm home.'

'No. It'll seem strange. My dad always tells me to think positive. No matter what the consequences. If you think positive even disappointments have a silver lining.'

'I don't think a broken heart can have a silver lining. But I'm trying to hang on to the most important part of it. Maybe I haven't let my soul go yet.' I smiled as Sam reached out and squeezed my arm.

'You'll survive, Carrie. You'll survive.'

She was right. I'd survive. But when the plane was landing I had to cling on to those words of hers. I felt nervous. I felt upset at having to say goodbye to Sam, although I had her address and phone number with me. We didn't have a long goodbye. We just gave each other a massive hug and just separated into the crowds before any of us could get all damn emotional.

For a while I just stood there, rather bemused. I felt kind of dumb standing there in the middle of everyone. Having watched Sam disappear. Well, that was the last stage. Seeing Sam go. The last stage before meeting Dad again. I was happy at the thought of seeing him but for obvious reasons that fact was kind of jaded, slightly. When should I tell Dad? What should I tell him? How? What? My heart was racing as I collected my gear from the lounge. My hands were shaking as I went through the 'Nothing to Declare' zone. There, God damn it, he was. I could see him. See him standing there in his leather jacket

Just for a moment I forgot. As I hugged Dad. As he seemed so happy to see me. For a moment I forgot about reality. But then, I guess, in a rush it came back to me. Just then Dad said he was surprised that I'd come home so soon.

'I can't tell you anything, Dad. Not until we get home, all right?'

He sensed something was wrong. I knew he sensed something was wrong. We talked on the way back. About life on the kibbutz. Just the fundamentals, that was all. He was keeping it under his hat, though. And I was keeping it under mine.

England looked so different. It was weird. It felt claustrophobic in a way. So much greenery around. Houses. Everything. It was beautiful in a way. Suddenly I thought of England as being beautiful and in a way, it made me glad to be back.

'I think I've taken it for granted,' I said, as we were nearing home.

'What's that, love?'

'England. Israel was good but I guess England's the best.'

'It's home.'

'Yes.'

'And you could paint?'

'I've done a bit of work, yes.'

'Good.'

'Is Zoe at home?'

'School.'

'You wouldn't give her a day, then?'

'No,' Dad smiled. 'She tried hard to get me round her finger though.'

'I thought she might do.' I smiled but I was thinking all the time. As we neared home. Thinking. Thinking. Thinking. How the hell was I going to tell him? How the hell?

In spite of it all I felt our house welcomed me somehow. It seemed to say, you're home, everything's going to be alright. It seemed to say that. I lugged all my stuff indoors while Dad was making a pot of tea. I knew the time was nearing. The time when Dad would be expecting an explanation. Something like. He came in with the tray. He poured the tea and then looked straight at me with those old, worldwise eyes of his.

'Carrie.' He said. 'Well, there's no point in getting wound up about what you have to tell me. Whatever it may be.'

I just stood there. In fact, nearly crying. It suddenly seemed all too much. The whole thing.

'Sit down, love,' Dad said.

I couldn't help crying. Having to face the reality with Dad. But knowing at the same time he was there. I was home. Not alone with the problem in Israel.

'Well, Carrie. What has happened?'

'I don't know how I'm going to tell you this, Dad. It's the hardest thing I've ever had to say to you.'

'How about taking a deep breath and coming right out with it?'

'I just want to say that I'm sorry. I didn't mean it to happen. I know what people are going to say.'

'I don't take any notice of people, you know that.'

'I'm pregnant, Dad. I'm pregnant.'

15

I just sat there with my own sobs. The reality of the whole situation breaking me in two. I didn't dare look at Dad. I felt so much that I'd let him down. Honest to God. I felt like he was going to lash out at me or something.

'Carrie, is that definite?' Dad's voice didn't even sound angry. But there was a touch of coarseness in it. A touch which said he was miffed. Just slightly miffed.

'Are you cross with me?' I knew he was and I felt like a five year old asking him that but the words just came out.

'You mean to say, Carrie. After all I've told you, you didn't take any precautions?'

'We used a condom but it split. It was the first time, Dad. It was my first time and I'm pregnant.'

'All right. All right. Just calm down.'

'You don't know how scared I was to tell you.'

'Well, it's come as a shock. But the thought had crossed my mind. The thought had crossed my mind.'

I wiped my eyes and blew my nose.

'Are you angry with me?'

'I'm just shocked, Carrie. Shocked, okay?'

'You are angry, I know.'

'It'll take a while to sink in? Who is he? The father.'

'He's a playwright. I might as well tell you now that he's forty years old.'

'Forty!!!!'

I nodded.

'Christ, what are you doing with a forty year old? I'm only forty three.'

'I love him, Dad. I do.'

'So, what's happening? Did he fly back with you? Is he English?'

'Yes, he's English. He's on his way to Greece. He travels around quite a bit. He's a professional playwright.

'I don't care if he's a professional dosser. Was he taking advantage of you?'

'No, I loved him. I still do love him.'

'So, when's he coming over here then?'

'I don't know.'

'Well, you must have arranged a date and decided what you're going to do.' Dad was getting more and more wound up. I could tell.

'No, Dad, it's not like that,' I half shouted, trying not to get hysterical but finding it hard not to.

'It's not like what?'

'We just haven't arranged anything.'

'Are you trying to tell me he doesn't want anything to do with you?'

'I don't know. I just don't know.'

'Of course you know. Just tell me.' Dad was shouting then. I just knew it would end up in a row.

'All right. He doesn't want anything to do with me. You might as well have the whole hog. The whole story. And you can just stuff it. I'm going out. I wish I hadn't even come back here. I wish that.'

'Come back, Carrie,' Dad yelled as I was on my way to the front door.

'Why should I come back. You were never around when I needed you anyway. I'll make a damn better mother than you ever did a father, I'll tell you that much.' I slammed the door as hard as I could and stormed past Dad's car. I just walked. Fast and hard down the street to the park. I felt like a fag but hadn't brought any with me. At least I'd stopped crying. This was it, I thought. Just the same as when I was ten years old. Running out on Dad. Running out. Running to the park. No Mum to run to. Never. No Mum to run to. So, the park was my mother. The park. Suddenly I thought of Sam. As I was sitting on one of the larger swings, I thought of Sam. I wished she was there, swinging back and forth with me. God, what a hassle. What a half bit hassle.

I stayed in the park for about an hour before I knew I'd have to go back. At least I felt a bit more in control of myself. I hoped Dad would be feeling the same way. I needed someone to tell me it would be all right. I really needed that. Just as I was walking from the park I saw Zoe. She met me. We hugged each other and she was crying a bit, crying because she was so happy to see me. We went back to the park and sat on one of the seats.

'Oh, Carrie! Carrie! Dad's okay. Honestly. We're glad to have you home, no matter what.'

'You know I'm pregnant.'

'He must be a great guy.'

'The reality is, he doesn't want to know me.'

'And to think you used to give me lectures. I should have been giving them to you. Anyway you've always wanted lots of children. What's the hassle?'

I had to smile then. Smile at my sister. At her nonchalant, carefree attitude.

'Come on, let's go home,' she said.

'Is Dad still in?'

'He's got to go at six. He's all right, though. I've had a chat to him.'

'Given him a lecture, have you?' I ruffled her shaggy locks.

'Well, somebody's got to sort our family out. What with you getting pregnant and Dad getting engaged.'

'What?' I stopped. Still.

'Yeah, well, sort of. Both Maddi and I are trying to talk him into it.'

'Maddi!!! The same Maddi?'

'Yeah, good old Maddi. She's actually given Dad an ultimatum. Marry me or piss off.'

I laughed.

'So, at the moment he's trying to make his mind up. I reckon there's going to be a marriage and a christening in the near future.'

'Well, that's a turn up, isn't it?'

'Maddi practically lives round our place now. She's great. She'll understand about you.'

'You are all right with her then?'

'Yeah. We have our ups and down, but, who doesn't. It's nice to have someone else's attention. You'll find it too. She'll be around when Dad's not.'

'Home again.'

'No hassle,' she repeated. I wished that life really was as simple as Zoe made it out to be. No hassle? As I went in I wished that with the whole of my heart.

16

Settling back down to a life of normality seemed quite weird after having been in Israel. Perhaps it would have been different if I wasn't actually pregnant. But even that was confirmed for me by a visit to my own doctor. After that the reality did hit me and perhaps I was even beginning to regret it. Knowing I couldn't start a detective agency. Well, that's what Dad reckoned, because I was pregnant. Although, I thought he was just making an excuse really. But, there again, what the hell was I meant to do? Who would have me work for them if they knew I was pregnant. No decent employer would have me. No, what I really wanted to do was this private detective business. That just seemed like a great challenge to me. It really did. But to do that even, I'd need a car or a motor bike. Something to get me round. And then I sometimes wondered if the whole thing was just a pipe dream or something. It was strange. I'd suddenly lost a lot of confidence. Since coming home again. All my confidence from long ago had vanished. I didn't know if it was because I was pregnant or because I was doing nothing at home and not being stimulated enough. I just didn't know.

To cap it all I wasn't having an exactly easy pregnancy either. I suffered terrible morning sickness. For about half an hour when I got up each morning I would be puking up in the loo. I'd been to the hospital to to see the midwife. She was a nice, motherly sort of woman but, by what she'd said I would just have to put up with the sickness. I'd gone to the hospital when I was eighteen weeks. She booked me in and took all the details. Then she gave me a blood test to see if my iron count was okay and also for a spina bifida check. I found out a few days later that everything concerning that was okay so I was relieved about that but even so, I still felt fed up. Mega fed up, in fact. I wrote letters to Sam, great, long, letters. Trying to eradicate my fears and work my life out through them. It helped a bit I suppose and her letters to me were encouraging. She had applied to join the policeforce and was now waiting to hear from them. Oh, I don't know, perhaps I felt envious of Sam then. Her life seemed so straight-forward and on the way up. Compared to hers, my life just seemed to be in one hell of a muddle. I was slowly sinking into a depression. A state of mind which I'd rarely been in before. It wasn't helped with the relationship I had with Dad. I still felt it was under strain. He had accepted it in a way but I still felt there was some unresolved tension between us. It was almost like we were living on a timebomb. One wrong word. One wrong action and it would explode. From both ends it would explode. I began to wish I could earn enough money to leave home. To just be on my own without the hassle of family around me. The only one who made me a tiny bit happy was Zoe. Well, I suppose there was Maddi too but I just didn't take to her in the same daughterly way that Zoe had. In some ways both of us were after the same man's affections. She did understand though and she tried to ease things a bit between Dad and I sometimes. Although, in the mood I was in, I wasn't particularly quick to be eased.

I guess half of it was my fault. I shouldn't have

been waiting for a letter from Cliff. I shouldn't have spent so much time dreaming that he'd write to me and suddenly turn up on the doorstep. For three solid months I'd been dreaming and as my baby grew inside me so did my passion at the thought of Cliff. Every morning, after the postman had been, I would go into a mega depression when there was no word from him. It made me irritable and moody. I just couldn't talk to Dad about it. He'd only get wound up which would make things even worse. It really was hell. The whole situation didn't seem to have any light shining on it at all. I'd also started to feel very tired so had taken to having an afternoon sleep as well, which was really unusual for me because as a rule I hated sleeping in the day. Sometimes it was just a relief though. To go to sleep. It made the day go quicker. I'd also started worrying about the baby inside me. I was due to have a scan in ten days time. All I kept thinking about was that something was wrong with the baby. I was becoming paranoiac as well as everything else. And that, I could definitely do without.

'Carrie, you've got to do something.' Maddi was sitting opposite me one Wednesday afternoon. Only her and I in the lounge. In fact she'd caught me listening to romantic records. 'You'll go crazy if you sit around here much longer. And that won't do you or the baby any good.'

I just looked down at my fingers. She was right. Somehow I had to pull myself together. For the baby's sake.

'That job in the newsagent is going,' Maddi said. It was a job as a shop girl in a newsagent-cum-post office. They'd told Dad I could begin whenever I wanted. It was a full-time job. Nine to five. 'It would be money,' Maddi continued. 'Then, perhaps you could get yourself a small car or something. You could go out more then. You could do the job for a few months anyway. Your Dad wouldn't expect much for housekeeping. The rest could all be savings.'

'I hate having to get jobs through Dad.'

'I know, love. Just think of it as a respite. Give yourself a break. Let your Dad do something for you. Like this job.'

I just looked at her. Wondering at what she'd said.

'He doesn't condemn you for being pregnant, Carrie. He blames himself for the state you're in now, though. He's worried about what will happen in the future. You have to show him your true spirit. Your true verve. Your get up and go.'

'You're wrong. He does condemn me for being pregnant. I've ruined it all, haven't I? I've ruined my whole freedom of life. Just for one stupid thing. Falling in love with one hell of a bastard. Just like Dad used to be. One hell of a bastard.'

'Are you going to throw that back at him, then?'

'Oh God, no. No, Maddi. I don't want to throw that at him.'

'But are you? By the way you're acting. You're shutting your Dad off, Carrie.'

'You mean he's shutting me off.' But half of me knew that wasn't really true. 'Oh, God, Maddi. I don't know anything. I feel so guilty that I've let everyone down. I don't know how to act with Dad. I just feel different now. I don't want to be at home any more. Once I've had the baby I'll have to find somewhere else. I really will. I won't put the baby up for adoption. I think if I stayed here, Dad would persuade me to. I'm not being spiteful, it's the truth.'

'Perhaps I can understand that. But perhaps if you give your Dad the chance to understand, he would too.'

'The thing is I never thought I'd have to grow up so quick. Being pregnant has made it all different. I can't be Dad's little girl, any more. I can't because I'm going to have my own baby. I'm going to be a mother. What I lost I'm going to be. Do you think I'm awfully selfish, Maddi? Having this baby?'

'I don't think you're being selfish, love,' Maddi leant over and took my hand. 'You'll love that child. I know you will. You'll love it and care for it and we'll all be there, Carrie. We'll all be there to help you, even if you are living on your own.'

'If he came, Maddie. If Cliff came now. I mean, if he did, I'd have him. I would, I'd have him back. I'd run to him. I'd love him.'

'Yes, I believe you would.'

'Dad wouldn't have that, though, would he?'

'I think your father would find that hard to understand. Although I think you've made it clear that you would have Cliff. If it happened perhaps your Dad would get used to the idea. Are you still hoping then?'

I sniffed. 'Well, I've just got this feeling. Just a feeling. We had such a strong bond between us. We really did.'

'But that doesn't mean you should mope around, waiting for him. You've got to start making your own life. Getting out a bit more. Making new friends. Seeing the old ones. Maybe if you met another fella?'

I smiled at that. 'If Cliff doesn't come, I'm going to give up on fellas altogether.'

'Well, at least I've got you smiling.'

'Oh, you're right, Maddi. I've got to do something or I'll drive myself mad.'

'What about the newsagent as step number one?'

'Okay.' I suddenly felt just a tiny bit happier. It was the first time I'd had a really good heart to heart with Maddi and with it, she'd made me feel better. Just by talking. 'I'll go and see them now,' I said.

'Say you'll start next Monday. That'll give you four clear days to get yourself sorted.'

Maddi turned out to be right. As soon as I'd secured the job with the postmaster, Fred, who I vaguely knew, I felt quite overjoyed. Just by having a job. Something to aim at. It was a weird feeling but it made me feel better just to think I'd have to get up in the morning and live by a routine once again. Plus I'd be earning cash. I was already thinking that perhaps I would save for a car. Perhaps I would. But then the thought of the baby put dampers on that one. I guess every penny I earned would have to go towards the baby. They cost. Or so I'd been told. Babies cost.

Sam rang that night with the news that she had got an interview with some nob to do with the policeforce. She was right chuffed about it. I told her about my job and she went on about me becoming a private detective.

'Well, you could get things started for when the baby is due,' she said. 'You know things like . . .'

'Sam, for the first nine months I'll be looking after the baby.'

'Well, after that you are going to work, aren't you? You're not going to be one of those stay-at-home mothers!!'

'Of course I'm not. I'd go crazy at home. But one thing at a time, you know?'

'So, that's when you could be a private Harry. About a year's time?'

'Well, yeah.'

'Will you still be living at home when you've had the baby?'

'I hope not.'

'Where else can you go?'

'I could get a council place.'

'Oh, whatever, you'll land up on your feet, so don't worry about it.'

'Thanks for the vote of confidence.' I had to laugh. Laugh along with Sam. It was great hearing from her. You know, suddenly everything seemed to be looking brighter. Just about everything did.

17

He gave it to me. Saturday morning. I'd been awake for half an hour but couldn't be bothered to actually get out of bed. Dad knocked on my door and came in. He had a letter for me.

'What's his name?' he said, dropping the letter on my bed where I could reach it. When I saw it was an airmail one my whole heart seemed to leap. I looked at Dad but he wasn't even smiling. Because of that I tried to calm myself down.

'Thanks, Dad,' I said.

'Are you getting up or do you want breakfast in bed?'

'It's all right, Dad, I'll be up.'

'I'll take Zoe's in then,' he disappeared and I just lay back for a while gazing at the letter. It was his handwriting. I knew it was from Cliff. I could recognize his spidery writing. His trademark. His career. His baby. His trademark. His career. His baby. I opened the letter. With my heart in my mouth, I opened the letter.

Dear Carrie,
As I promised you I am flying back to England in two days time. I was under the impression that you thought I'd go forever. I couldn't think of any way of putting your mind at rest. I miss you practically every day. I miss you and I wonder how you and how our baby are. I'll be living at my flat in Kensington, the phone

number is at the top of the page. It's up to you whether you phone or not. I would like to marry you. To do everything properly. I wouldn't say that if I didn't love you and think that we could have a life together. To create our own family.

By the time you receive this letter I shall be in London just waiting for your call. I shall try and understand if you no longer want or need me. I have prayed, though. Prayed that our love has lasted through all the trauma of the past few months.

Well, Carrie, this is just a short letter. I shall be waiting to hear from you in much anticipation. Until then, I send all my love to you.

Constantly thinking of you,
Cliff.

I just lay there. The pages of the letter scattered on my bed in front of me. You wouldn't believe it. I mean, I couldn't believe it. Although I'd hoped and dreamt and had visions of him writing a letter to me. Of my having a change of heart. I knew I'd ring Cliff. I'd already forgiven him. I loved him that much and I still did. I still felt we were right for each other and what Cliff had done hadn't changed that.

I felt immensely happy again. Truly happy, but I realized things weren't going to be that simple. At least, my financial situation would be settled if I married Cliff. I mean Cliff had no worries over money and neither would I have as his wife. Neither our baby. Our own, special baby. Suddenly something leapt in my stomach and I put my hand on it. Was it the baby? Was it the baby of the father? Was it? Leaping in anticipation. I was thinking then. I could even start my own detective agency. Carry on with my painting too. Oh, suddenly the whole world seemed to be at my feet.

As I was having a shower I felt slightly calmer and realized once again that it wasn't going to be that simple. I mean, there was Dad, for a start. There was Dad. A definite hurdle. He knew how old Cliff was and he'd been against that fact all along. In fact, I would have to handle the whole situation with soft hands. If I could. Without getting too wound up myself. If I could. I was beginning to become quite nervous at the prospect, though as I got changed and, sitting at my dressing table, combed through my wet hair, I somehow wished that Maddi had stayed overnight. I thought she would have been able to help matters if she'd been with us. Especially where Dad was concerned. Still, she wasn't there and Zoe never surfaced until midday on a Saturday, so she wouldn't be helping me much. I knew it was only going to be me and Dad.

I took a deep breath and crossed my fingers. Well, I'd have to do it. I'd have to tell Dad of the latest situation. No matter what, I'd have to tell him.

I slowly went downstairs, after putting Cliff's letter together and placing it underneath my mattress for safety. I slowly went downstairs and into the kitchen.

Dad was sitting at the bar reading the *Independent*. I just went past him to fetch the kettle and fill it with water. Dad said nothing but by the tense look on his face, I feared that he'd realized the letter had been from Cliff and that he wasn't too pleased. I poured some muesli into a bowl and filled a glass with orange juice. I added the milk to the muesli. I knew Dad was making it difficult for me by not saying anything. Not trying to clear the air which made it all the more difficult for me. I knew I'd have to start. I'd have to say something. I'd just have to.

'Dad?' I began.

'Em?' With his head still buried in the paper.

'Dad, that letter was from Cliff.'

'Yes. I did gather.'

'Well, can we talk? Can you stop reading the paper?'

He looked up then. Saying nothing.

'We've got to talk Dad, all right? Cliff wants to marry me. He's back in England. Look Dad, I know you're not going to understand this but I've forgiven Cliff. I've forgiven him for how he treated me. I still love him, Dad. I want to marry him.'

'Oh, it's that simple, is it? He just pleads in a letter and you go running back to him. Well, that goes to show you're too immature to get married. If you were mature you'd see Cliff for what he is. I presume he's gay, is he? Most of these playwrights are.'

I just stood there. Just taking all Dad's words and trying to stay calm. I couldn't, though. I just couldn't make it.

'Christ, Dad. You're a right one to talk. I don't forget our mother, you know. I don't forget how she died. Because she couldn't take any more of your abuse. Think I've forgotten that, do you? Well, I haven't. I haven't. You've got no right to preach to me. We pulled you out of it. Me and Zoe. We took you back, didn't we? We forgave you.'

'Can't you see!! That's the point,' Dad suddenly shouted. Slamming his hands down on the bar.

Making me jump. 'You're just going from me to him, aren't you? Making the classic example. Your mother's father was an alcoholic, so she married an alcoholic. Me. Yes. I remember, Carrie. I remember every damn morning. You told me this guy used to be an alcoholic. Well, Christ, that's the same pit, isn't it? The same trap. He'll abuse you like I abused your mother. Can't you see what I'm getting at? I made your mother pregnant. That's why she married me. Now, the same has happened to you. Can't you see that? Well, can't you?'

I just stood there. In shock. I never knew. I'd never known that the reason Mum and Dad got married was because she was pregnant.

'Was it me?' I said, trying at the same time to work things out in my own mind. 'Dad, was it me?'

'Well, who the hell do you think it was?'

I just walked out. I had to. Because I couldn't cope with it. I couldn't cope with the news. It hurt. It stung inside when it shouldn't really have done. But, to find that out. To find out I was illegitimate. Suddenly. And now the circle turns. Now the circle turns. In my turmoil I could suddenly understand why Dad had been acting how he had. It must have brought it all back to him. Mum, Zoe and I. Dad being an alcoholic. Mum committing suicide. And the guilt. The awful guilt that Dad felt. I suddenly understood. It must have been hard. Hard for Dad when he knew I was pregnant. Especially by a man who used to be an alcoholic. By a man who had treated me badly, just as badly as Dad used to treat me.

I lay on my bed and cried. Crying into my pillow. For the whole hog of it. I'd never known I was the reason Mum and Dad got married. But perhaps I can understand it now. Understand it because I'm pregnant now. I'm not getting married because I'm pregnant, though. I'm getting married because I love Cliff. I love him. Oh, I cried. I cried because sometimes life seemed so difficult. So difficult and hard. It really did.

18

About half an hour later there was a knock on my door. I'd stopped crying but was just lying on my bed, thinking.

'Carrie?' Dad poked his head around the door. I looked at him.

'Can I come in, Carrie?'

'Yeah.' By the tone of Dad's voice he had calmed down a bit. He didn't seem angry any more. He came in and sat on my bed.

'It's true, Carrie. Everything I said.'

'I didn't want to bring the past up but you made me. I love Cliff, Dad. I really love him.'

'I know, you must do.'

'But I can understand how you feel and I don't know what to say to make things easier.'

'Maybe I've just got to have faith, eh. You're not six years old any more. You're a very beautiful young woman. You've been making your own decisions for years and that was because of me. Okay? I know that. I just don't want to see you go. I guess we didn't have too many years together, did we?'

'Oh, Dad,' I wrapped my arms around him. 'It's not your fault. We can still have each other. We can still make up for lost time. I won't be going far. You'll like Cliff, Dad. Somehow you've got a lot in common. Good things, I mean. Good things.'

'Good things.' Dad smiled as if he couldn't believe in any good things. It was odd. Just like we were all doomed to destruction. Well, were we? Was it right to be optimistic or wasn't it? I suddenly felt fed up. Dad looked depressed all of a sudden. Almost as if us two making friends again had been too much for him.

'Dad, I am going to be okay, you know.'

'I trust you will be. Anyway, it's not the end of the world. Even for your mother it wasn't the end of the world. On this earth, maybe, but . . .'

'Do you believe that, Dad?'

'Sometimes it's a case of having to believe it.'

'I don't want to make you unhappy. But you won't be. Not once you meet Cliff. I know there's an age gap but maybe I need that. Maybe I do.'

'So, what's the next move?'

'I'll have to phone him and invite him here.'

'And you'll live happily ever after.'

'Dad!!!'

'Yeah, I'm sorry. I can't get used to the idea that you're really leaving the nest.'

'We've always been independent, Dad. Even Zoe. You've got to think of you now. Maddi. What you're going to do. Think of your life.'

'Yes.'

'We could get married together.'

'Thanks, love, but I wouldn't spoil your day. I wouldn't do that at all.'

'Well, we'll both have our days then.'

'Maddi and I won't be getting married just yet.'

'Well, don't keep her waiting too long.'

'I know. I know. She's happy for the moment, anyway. Well, reckon you've got a phone call to make.'

'Yeah.'

'No more tears then, eh?' Dad got up and held out his hand to pull me from the bed. I knew I could trust Dad then. I knew I could trust him with Cliff and that was the main thing. It really was.

Suddenly my mood swung yet again. From depression to happiness. All of a sudden I swung. I felt happy again and suddenly the thought of Cliff made my heart beat fast. I took the note from under my mattress and took it downstairs. One phone was in the kitchen and one was in Dad's room. I decided to use Dad's because it was more private.

'It's all right, I won't disturb you,' Dad followed me into his room. 'I won't disturb you. Just getting my jacket.'

'You going out?'

'Down town. Tell Zoe.'

'See you later.'

I just sat on Dad's bed. Just sat on it, looking down at the phone. I suddenly felt nervous. Really nervous and half paranoid. I mean I felt so close to Cliff then but fear made me seem so far as well. It was difficult. I was scared to make the phone call and, in a way, after having received the letter that was irrational.

Do it. I chided myself. Do it now. Trying to be firm I quickly picked up the receiver and began dialling the number.

It rang. It kept on ringing. No one answered. My heart was going ten to the dozen and my hands were clammy, holding on to the phone. Three more rings, I thought. Three more rings and then I'll give up.

It was answered on the second ring.

'Hello. Cliff Maynard speaking.'

His voice. Just to hear his voice. So close to me. So soft. So gentle. But with a kind of authority about it. A professional's authority.

'Who is this, please?'

'It's Carrie,' I managed to speak. There was silence on the other end. Neither of us spoke for a short while. I just didn't know what to say.

'Carrie,' he finally spoke. 'How are you? Did you get the letter? Well, of course. You must have done. Christ, it was so simple, Carrie. I can't believe this. You must have a heart. A real heart.'

'Faith,' I said.

'I need it, Carrie. I need you. It's that simple.'

'Are you coming down?'

'I've got your address. I'll start off after lunch. I know where it is. I looked it up on the map.'

'You won't get lost then.'

'Probably, but I'd do it for you.'

'I don't know what to say, Cliff. I mean, you ran out on me. Do you want our baby? I have to know by word that you want our baby.'

'I do, Carrie. But you come first, not the baby. Not at the moment.'

'All right, come down.'

'Will your father mind?'

'You'll both have to tread carefully, okay.'

'That's understandable. I let you down, didn't I.'

'We'll talk when you get here.'

'Of course. I'll see you later then.'

'Drive carefully.'

'Bye.'

It was a weird feeling. In a way it was almost as if Cliff and I hadn't split. As if we hadn't been apart for months. It was strange. I felt lightheaded. I felt the baby inside me. Does it matter, I thought. Baby. Our baby. Does it matter? Cliff used to be an alcoholic. He used to be. I thought of Dad's words earlier, then I thought of Mum. Of her father who was an alcoholic too. Do children always go astray as their parents before them went astray? Is that the truth? I suddenly felt panic. At the thought of a baby growing inside me. At the thought of marrying someone whom I hardly knew. What was so special about Cliff, anyway? Was it just infatuation? Would he start drinking again? Would he? Would he abuse me like Dad abused Mum? I sat on Dad's bed feeling gut sick. It was almost as if the whole episode of Israel in my life had suddenly been wiped out. Just like that. No go. Zero. No number. For God's sake, what the hell am I doing with my life? I felt scared. I felt very scared. My feelings happened to change. My feelings towards Cliff. It had all seemed so illuminating in Israel. So full of verve and spirit. But then, then there was nothing. Really nothing. I suddenly felt devoid of feeling. I felt devoid of any passionate feeling for Cliff at all.

19

I cooked the lunch. Just to keep my mind occupied. I made a chicken casserole with white sauce. I had just put it in the oven when Zoe decided to show herself.

'When's lover boy getting here then?' She poured herself an orange juice. She hadn't got changed. Half past midday and she was still in her nightclothes.

'How do you get all this information, darling?'

'Dad told me. Well, aren't you hysterically happy?'

'Zoe, its not all love and roses you know. It's not all up in the air. Like some gigantic gas filled balloon. One has to be realistic you know. Realistic.'

'You know, Dad once told me I was very perceptive.'

I looked at her, slightly annoyed. I grabbed the kettle and in rather a rush I filled it with water.

'Did you hear what I said?' Zoe half whined, which really grated at me then.

'I know you're perceptive, Zoe. I know.'

'Cold feet, eh?'

'What!!!'

'Sorry.'

'Zoe, just spit it out if you've got something to say.'

'I just said it. Cold feet, I said. Why can't we just talk without getting wound up? You're so much on the defensive just lately.'

'Well, what the hell do you expect? If you were pregnant and single you'd be on the defensive as well.'

'Loads of single girls get pregnant.'

'Oh, yeah? It's quite common, is it?'

'I didn't mean common like that.'

'I'm having an illegitimate child,' I yelled. Not being able to control myself any longer. 'I'm having a bastard in other words. A bastard. How d'you think I feel about that? I was a bastard. Did you know that? Mum and Dad got married because she was pregnant with me. Now, the circle has turned.'

'Cliff's not still an alcoholic is he?'

'How the hell do I know?' But Zoe, as usual, had the habit of getting to the point. Straight there. Do not pass go and do not collect five hundred. Something like that anyway.

'Are you scared he'll be like Dad was?'

'I've got no choice, Zoe. I have to marry Cliff.'

'Of course you don't have to. I mean it. That's what I was trying to say. But that's not the problem, is it? If you think that he's still an alcoholic, well, that's a different matter. Did he sound drunk on the phone then?'

'No.'

'Why then? If you weren't worried in Israel.'

'Things just go in circles, that's all. It'll be just my luck to marry an alcoholic bastard.'

'O, catch out, babe. You're right screwed up today.'

'I just don't know if I can do it. I don't know where I am. All I know is that I'm pregnant. All I'm thinking of now is all those things I won't be able to do because I've got a child.'

'If you marry Cliff, though. If you do then you'll be able to do what the hell you like. He has got the money.'

'Be tied, have money. Be free, be broke.'

'That's good.'

'Maybe I'd rather be free and broke.'

'Maybe it will be okay when Cliff gets here.'

'What about if I don't love him any more?'

'I guess you'd just call it a day.'

'Would it really be that simple?'

'Of course it would. That simple.'

I smiled then. Just as the water was ready for coffee. Oh, hell. If Zoe could still make it sound simple then I must be getting bloody old and senile or something. Old and damn senile. And that fact was damn simple too.

We had our lunch, Dad, Zoe and I. Maddi was up London on business. 'I have left some for Maddi, Dad. She can just heat it up.'

'Okay. Thanks. Listen, d'you want us to be out when Cliff gets here? Just to get some privacy.'

'Aren't you working then?'

'Not until six.'

'Oh, don't worry about it, he's got to meet you anyway.'

'Well, Zoe and I are going out at half three anyway. Aren't we Zoe?'

'Are we?'

Dad nodded energetically at her.

'We are,' she said.

'Thanks.' I looked at Dad.

They went out. I was left alone in the house so I made myself look presentable. A large skirt, best tee shirt and best cardigan. Dad reckoned Cliff would make it by four. When four showed on the clock I was trembling. I walked up and down the hallway. Constantly stopping at the window to see if I could see a car. I was really mad at myself for getting in such a state. But I couldn't calm down. I really couldn't.

When I saw the silver Mercedes I thought it was

one of Dad's friends for a minute. But suddenly I glimpsed him. Cliff, in the car. I could recognize his curly hair. Even from the house I could practically see the aura which always went with him. This is true, I thought. This is true. Cliff is actually here. Part of me wanted to dash out to him. Just so that I could give him a massive great hug. I resisted the temptation, though. I waited until he was walking down the drive and then I flew to the front door and opened it for him.

I did then. I opened the door for Cliff.

20

We were transfixed. Both of us were. We just stood gazing into each others eyes. I saw all the warmth and the love in Cliff that I'd seen before. Also all the serenity. All the peace. The calmness. The person inside Cliff which said, it's all right, I am here, I will look after you. You are precious to me. All that and more. Suddenly we were in each others arms. This is what I'd dreamt about. How I'd dreamt of it since returning from Israel.

We stood there in the hallway kissing and hugging, feeling each other. Then Cliff lead me into the lounge and shut the front door.

'Oh, Cliff. I'm so happy.'

'But you cry a few tears?'

'You know I was thinking terrible things earlier on today. Things like I no longer loved you. Maybe I didn't even like you. Cliff, I'm going to have your baby. Do you want the baby? Do you want me?'

'Carrie, how many times will you ask me? Can't you trust now? Because I let you down once, can't you trust?'

'It's just all so unbelievable.'

'It's what you want. Not me but you.'

'I will be a working mother, Cliff. I have to be. But I've always wanted to be a young mother too.'

'I can feel no objection to that. Don't cry, Carrie. I'm the one who should be crying.'

'You just got cold feet. You weren't sure. You needed time to think.'

'All those things, but I was being cowardly.'

'Did you drink?'

'What?'

'Alcohol. I mean,' I'd just said it off the cuff. I knew he hadn't been drinking again. I trusted that he hadn't. But then the way he suddenly turned away from me. He turned away and walked to the window. It suddenly hit me. He had been drinking. He had been drinking alcohol again. Suddenly disappointment ran through my body like the blood running through my veins.

'Oh, Cliff.'

'You've got to have faith in me, Carrie.'

'I did have faith in you.' But it had been spoilt. All of it. My vision had been spoilt.

'You have to trust me as I am. I won't drink like I used to drink. Not a bottle a day. I won't do that. But I felt pressure. I just did it. I couldn't talk, I just had to drink.'

It was weird. Suddenly it seemed as if I was in a time warp. It wasn't Cliff standing there, it was Dad. I wasn't eighteen years old, I was eight years old. And they were the same words. Practically the same words.

Cliff came to kiss me. He shouldn't have done. I could taste alcohol on his kiss. That which I hadn't noticed before. In all my excitement I could have missed the most important fact then about Cliff.

'When did you have your last drink?' I asked him.

'Three days ago.' He was also a cowardly liar, I turned away from his arms. My stomach sinking fast. I was suddenly feeling spaced out.

'You're a liar,' I half whispered.

'Carrie!!! What!!!'

'You're a liar. You've had some today, haven't

you?' I spoke louder, turning on him as I did so.

'Oh Christ, Carrie. I needed one today.'

'One? Bottle you mean?'

'I just stopped off in a pub, that's all. I just needed a booster. One glass. That's all.'

'Why the hell should I believe you?'

'Everyone's got their faults. I'm not perfect, Carrie. I don't claim to be.'

'I've got to know, Cliff. I don't want to go through it all again. I don't want it to be my father all over again. That's what I'm scared of.'

'I do understand you, Carrie. But you can't let your past life warp your judgement or you'd be too scared to go out the front door.'

'Are you saying, if I turned you away now you wouldn't go and get tanked up? I've seen it, Cliff. I've seen it all.'

'You're mature for your age Carrie, and I know why. Because you had to try and hold your family together. But are you going to let your father ruin your own future? Memories of the bad times. Can't you think only of the good times you've had since?'

'But what a sacrifice. What a sacrifice for a few, for a few good years. Maybe I'm not so mature Cliff because, just at this moment, I can't let go of my past.'

'Won't you give me a chance? Won't you give us a chance? Our baby?'

I didn't know. I just didn't know. I felt in complete and utter turmoil. All I wanted to do was to be alone. That was all. All. All. All. I suddenly screamed. Hysterically. Somehow the confusion and everything just seemed too much. I let go. I screamed. Then I flopped down on the settee. Cliff looked scared. Really frightened. Perhaps it was then. That very moment I knew

I couldn't go through with it. I could see the only security Cliff could ever find was through drink. Maybe he's not still an alcoholic. Maybe he would be a proper husband. Maybe. Maybe. Maybe. Oh, I just felt phased. I damn well knew then that as far as relationships went Cliff was a no hoper. All the heights of emotion. Of seeing him again. All the fantasies and dreams I'd had of him. I'd been right, hadn't I? I'd been right when I'd told Zoe that love wasn't like a great, gas filled, balloon, soaring high in the sky. I should have listened to my own advice when I was getting high. I really should have done.

Cliff was just standing in the middle of the room. He was shaking. Quivering, like some great, overgrown, school boy.

'*Carrie?*' He half whispered.

'You'll have to pay me maintenance, Cliff. For the baby. I'll let you see it. I will share our child with you if that's what you want. About the payments and that I'll have to see a solicitor. Perhaps it just wasn't meant to be.'

'Is that your final decision?'

'Yes.'

'I'll be able to give you a substantial payment. I'll go through my solicitor. A lump sum. Perhaps it would be better for the child.'

'We'll have to work it out. I'll give you my phone number.'

'Yes. Do that. We can work it out fairly. I don't want you or the baby to want for anything, Carrie.'

Suddenly Cliff seemed to change. When all the pressure was off him, it was almost like his change of mood was like a great sigh of relief from him. At the decision I'd come to. I had to smile really. Damn ironical.

'Carrie?'

I looked at him.

'You're not ready for marriage, are you?'

'It seems I'm ready for a baby.'

'Will you love the child?'

'Israel's babe. If it's a girl I shall call her Isrania.'

'At one stage I thought it could work. That I could take the extra commitment. But my first marriage broke down. I couldn't look after my daughter. I couldn't be a father and a husband. Believe me, Carrie, you're doing the right thing. You'll meet someone better. Who won't need alcohol. You'll meet someone who you can love securely. Who won't let you down,' He knelt by me and stroked my hair.

'Well sometimes, perhaps you could do me a favour and babysit.'

'I never got the hang of changing nappies.'

'If you're going to keep going around making girls pregnant you're going to have to learn to change nappies.'

'You're happier now. I can feel it.'

'Maybe we'll both grow up one day. D'you want a cup of tea or coffee? You can take down the phone number from the kitchen.'

It seemed a great weight had been lifted off both our shoulders. I made him coffee and a couple of sandwiches. Then we both chatted about things in general.

'How is your work? Your painting,' he asked, shoving the last piece of a sandwich into his mouth.

'I reckon you'd turn every one into an artist if you could.'

'Only if there's talent.'

'Just having talent is no good, Cliff. You have to have fortitude as well. I haven't been endowed with that gift, I'm afraid. A true artist should think his art is the most special thing in his life. I can't think that about art, Cliff. I can't be that committed. Not like you and your writing.'

'Well, at least you're honest, and that too is a gift. Will you really call her Isrania?'

'Of course I will.'

'I like that name.'

I reached over and put my hand over his as it was positioned on the table.

'Well,' he said. 'It's half-five. I'd better go. Before your father returns.'

'Frightened he'll beat you up, are you?'

'No. Its just that my tax is out of date on my four wheels out there.'

I had to laugh at that. 'Well my dad would probably lock you up for that so you'd better go quick.'

'Good luck with your job, Carrie. We'll stay friends.'

He went. With a quick kiss from me. I stood outside watching him drive away. It was odd. I breathed a sigh and felt better. I felt altogether better. Oh, I guess it might have worked. It might have done. But then Cliff wasn't strong. And I'm not about to support another weak man. I felt better that I'd seen him though, and that we'd both talked easily to each other. I would have hated us to have parted on a row or argument.

I went indoors and patted my stomach. 'Whatever you are,' I said, 'Whatever you are, girl or boy, you must know who your father is. And that, in his way, he loves you. He loves you very much indeed. Just like my own father. In his very own way, he loved me also.' I closed my eyes. Taking in the peace and the steadiness of a decision made. I rocked on the rocker. Lulled myself to sleep.

Rock a bye. Rock.